Hell in Paradise

Ex-sheriff Jed Grayson is on his way to Wyoming when he stops at the township of Paradise to rest for a few days. At the Golden Nugget Saloon he has an altercation with Zach Bassett, the son of the wealthiest rancher in the territory. Beating Zach to the draw, he humiliates the youngster in front of the saloon's patrons.

Zach gets even: enlisting the help of friends, he beats Jed to within an inch of his life. Recovering from his injuries, Jed vows to repay Zach for his crime, earning the enmity of the boy's father; the latter is waging a private war against the Thornton family, who own the second biggest ranch in Paradise. Events escalate as, forced by circumstances to throw in his lot with the Thornton family, Jed finds himself the target of a hired killer and has to fight to save his life.

Hell in Paradise

Pete B. Jenkins

A Black Horse Western

ROBERT HALE

© Pete B. Jenkins 2019
First published in Great Britain 2019

ISBN 978-0-7198-3009-9

The Crowood Press
The Stable Block
Crowood Lane
Ramsbury
Marlborough
Wiltshire SN8 2HR

www.bhwesterns.com

Robert Hale is an imprint
of The Crowood Press

Typeset by
Derek Doyle & Associates, Shaw Heath
Printed and bound in Great Britain by
4Bind Ltd, Stevenage, SG1 2XT

For my father Bryan Raymond Jenkins,
from one cowboy to another

CHAPTER ONE

Jed Grayson sat astride his black gelding with his hands resting on the saddle horn as he vainly tried to stretch the kinks out of his travel-weary back. The town sprawling out across the valley below looked mighty inviting to a man who had spent the past three weeks sleeping beneath the stars eating nothing but beans and drinking bad coffee.

The name on the marker beside the road said the town was called Paradise, and Jed figured that was good enough for him. With a gentle nudge he urged the gelding forward, eager to make the town's acquaintance.

The hot July sun shone down mercilessly on his battered brown Stetson as he made his way down the winding road to meet the outskirts of the pleasantly situated town – and given that it had been beating down on him for the past ten days or so, he was under no illusions as to his need for a bath and a change of clothes.

The sign he had just passed as he approached the town's first building informed him that the citizens of the good city of Paradise numbered 3,262 souls all told, so that was promising for finding not only a bathhouse, but a comfortable place to lodge for a few days, while he washed away the trail dust and rested not only his horse but his own weary body.

The gelding's hoofs cut out a hypnotic beat on the drought-hardened street while little eddies of dust swirled around its fetlocks as Jed Grayson made his way towards the centre of town. Nobody seemed to be paying him no mind as they scuttled here and there on that busy road going about their daily business. Judging by the angle of the sun it was just gone one o'clock, and Jed's rumbling stomach was giving him the message that it wanted to be filled. It was a toss-up whether he should bath first or fill his belly. But as the smell of freshly baked bread drifted down the street to assault his nostrils the prospect of a good feed pushed the idea of a hot bath from his mind for the time being.

A sign advertising hot meals with bread and coffee caught his eye, so riding over to the small café that promised such a luxury he eased his sore body out of the saddle and planted his size eleven feet on the hard surface of Paradise's main thoroughfare. Wrapping the gelding's reins around the hitching rail he stepped up on to the boardwalk and made for the front door.

A pretty young woman looked up as the tinkling bell on the café door rang out its invitation, and she smiled engagingly at him. 'You look as though you could do with a good square meal inside you.'

He smiled back, 'You don't know the half of it, ma'am.'

She showed him to a table over in the corner away from the window where the hustle and bustle outside would only serve to remind him of how tired he was, and waited to take his order.

'Steak, eggs, bacon, potatoes . . . dang it, why not just give me the works.'

'You leave it to me. I know just what you want,' she assured him then disappeared into another room to rustle it all up.

Jed placed his Stetson on the chair beside him and did his best to smooth down his grimy black hair. He caught a glimpse of himself in the glass of a cabinet that stood with its back up against the wall, its shelves stacked high with patterned crockery that had seen many years of service, and shuddered at the sight that jumped out at him. Haggard and looking well beyond his thirty-two years, he was in dire need of a tidy up. A haircut and shave would have to accompany that bath he was planning on taking if he was going to achieve anything even closely resembling respectability. He might just nip down to the saloon for a drink first though, as he hadn't touched a drop of whiskey since he had let his only bottle slip from his hand and smash on some rocks in a river he was crossing two weeks or so back. He was no boozer by a long way, but he had to admit he did like a decent shot of the stuff every couple of days, so by now he was holding out for a few stiff snorts of the fiery liquid.

'That was quick,' he said, as the waitress returned with a plate fair overflowing with all the grub a hungry man could wish for.

'I had most of it on the stove ready to go,' she confessed as she placed the plate on the table before him.
'If you want anything else then just holler, I'll be out the
back washing up.'

Jed attacked the banquet with gusto. He couldn't
remember the last time he had been served up such a
repast as this. It was almost enough to tempt him to find
himself a woman and settle down, although he had no
desire to repeat the debacle he had experienced with
Belinda. Belinda Carrington . . . now there was a name
and a woman he didn't care to remember. She had used
him for all he was worth and then tossed him away as if
he were nothing more than yesterday's newspaper.
When she had left town with that fast-talking gambler
he had to admit that it had hurt, and hurt bad – though
he fancied he was over her now, even if he hadn't quite
forgotten how it felt. Being left all alone with only his
sheriff's badge to give him any sense of self-respect had
brought on the wanderlust in him, so when his uncle
wrote to him inviting him to travel to Wyoming to help
on the spread he had bought for himself, Jed had
jumped at the chance to leave the town and his heart-
break behind. And now here he was, on the verge of
something new, and he wished for all it was worth that
this time he would be able to carve out a little happiness
for himself that would last.

When he was finished Jed left some money on the
table for the meal with a little something extra for the
pretty girl before stepping back outside to find a
saloon. He hadn't gone more than thirty yards when he
spotted what he was looking for. An imposing building

10

with The Golden Nugget written in bold letters above its batwing doors told him that a good time was waiting for him within its walls, so he quickened his step, eager to partake of its delights.

The smell of tobacco and cheap whiskey rushed to greet him the second he parted the batwings and his six foot two frame stepped across the threshold. After more days in the saddle than he cared to count, he was back where he belonged.

'What'll it be, mister?' A slim, slightly balding bartender stopped his polishing of the oak counter and waited patiently for Jed's answer.

'A whiskey . . . the best you've got.'

'Coming right up,' he left his rag on the counter and reaching up onto a shelf behind him, brought down a half empty bottle then uncorked it. 'You'll like this stuff. It costs more'n the usual stuff we serve but I reckon once you've tasted it you'll agree it's worth it.' Expertly pouring it out into a glass he slid it across the counter to Jed so he could sample it.

Picking the glass up Jed held it up at eye level and swilled it around a little, then putting the glass to his lips he threw it down his throat in one swift movement. The fiery liquid burned a pleasant pathway all the way down to his stomach, leaving a delightful taste in his mouth well after it had vacated that particular vicinity.

The bartender smiled with satisfaction. 'What did I tell you?'

'You weren't lying,' Jed said, returning the smile. He pulled some money out of his trouser pocket and slapped it down on the bar. 'How about leaving the bottle?'

11

Jed was lost in his thoughts when a young man sidled up to him and started to speak. He didn't catch what he said. 'What was that?' he asked, turning to look at the youngster.

'I said, are you working for Thomas Thornton?'

Jed looked the fellow over. A tad over six feet, he was pale in complexion with a head of carrot-red hair that resembled a well-used mop. His clear blue eyes blazed with a type of intensity that told Jed he was used to throwing his weight around to get what he wanted.

'Never heard of him,' Jed said truthfully.

The kid looked down at the low-slung gun on Jed's hip and then back at Jed's face again. 'You better not be lying to me, mister. If you are working for him it won't go well for you.'

Jed considered his remark silently for a moment. What business was it of this snot-nosed little punk who he decided to work for anyway?

'I think you'd better go back and join your friends,' he said eventually.

The boy's face clouded over. He obviously wasn't used to being spoken to in such a manner. 'Boys,' he called over his shoulder, 'I think we've got Thornton's new gunny here.'

So that was how it panned out. The kid thought Jed was some hired gun that this Thomas Thornton character had put on his payroll to do who knows what to who knows who. Maybe he should have left his Navy Colt in his saddlebags before he came in here. Folks were always assuming he was a gunman when they saw the pearl handled shooting iron sitting low on his hip.

Several chairs scraped the floor of the Golden Nugget in unison as the kid's friends got up to make their way over to join him at the bar.

'This here saddle bum's working for Thornton for sure,' the kid said as his pals looked Jed up and down.

'That right, mister?' one of them demanded.

'No it ain't,' Jed said calmly. 'Not that I reckon it's any business of yours.'

'He's a lippy one,' the kid said, a distasteful sneer forcing his top lip to curl up slightly.

'I'm the one who's in here for a quiet drink. It's you who came over here shooting your mouth off, not the other way around.'

'It's almost certain he's working for Thornton, Zach. Look how he wears his gun,' one of the men commented.

'That right, mister, you a gunfighter that Thornton's hired?'

Jed's patience was wearing thin. 'Why don't you boys run along and play your little game someplace else.'

'I think Pa would want us to take care of this bum, fellers. You know how he feels about Thornton hiring gunnies.'

'We're with you, Zach,' one of the men assured him.

'Hand over your gun,' Zach said aggressively.

Jed placed his glass down on the counter. 'Why don't you try and take it.'

The kid was quick, he had to give him that, but he wasn't in Jed's league, and so he was caught with his six-gun clear of the holster but the barrel pointing at the floor.

13

'Now I reckon so far as the law goes I've got the right to pull my trigger on you seeing as you drew on me first,' Jed said calmly, his Colt pointed right at the young man's chest. 'But I've never been one for sense-less killing if I can help it, so I'm gunna give you the chance to walk on out of here, and nothing more needs to be said about it.'

The kid glared at him in unbridled fury, it wasn't hard to see he would dearly love to finish his draw and put a hole right through this stranger who had humili-ated him in front of his friends, and he would have done just that if he thought he had a chance of pulling it off. 'Come on, boys,' he said as he let the pistol slip back into its holster, 'I reckon Pa is gunna be mighty interested to hear this feller's in town.'

'Any idea who that young punk is?' Jed asked the bar-tender after the kid and his sidekicks had left.

The bartender scowled. 'That's Zach Bassett, Jason Bassett's boy. Born with a silver spoon in his mouth, was that one. Thinks he's a cut above everyone else because his pa owns the biggest ranch in the territory.'

'He's gunna get himself killed if he doesn't watch his mouth.'

'I was kinda hoping you were gunna deal to him,' the bartender confessed. 'You woulda saved me a whole heap of trouble if you hadda.' He leaned in a little closer as if he didn't want anyone else to hear. 'He's torn this place up on more than one occasion, and for no other reason than he couldn't handle his whiskey.'

'I know the type. Fellers like him tend to live fast and die young.'

14

The bartender chuckled, 'I can only live in hope.'

'You wouldn't happen to know where I can find a room for a couple of days would you?' Jed asked, wishing to forget about the boy and his no good friends so he could see to his more immediate needs.

'There's a boarding house about halfway down the street, run by an old girl everyone calls Grandma Alice. The rooms are comfortable enough and the food is good.'

'Cheap?'

'The cheapest you'll find in town.'

'Sounds like the place for me.' Scooping his bottle off the bar he nodded to the bartender before heading for the batwings in search of Grandma Alice's place.

CHAPTER TWO

The boarding house door opened on Jed's seventh knock. As the heavy oak door creaked open on its rusty hinges he was given his first peek at the old woman affectionately known in Paradise as Grandma Alice.

'Yes?' she said, peering round the door at him through rheumy eyes.

Whipping his hat off Jed delivered her one of his best smiles. 'I was told by the bartender down at the Golden Nugget that there were rooms to be had here.'

She looked him up and down for a moment in a manner that told him she didn't approve of what she saw. 'I only take in respectable people.'

'I realize I'm looking a mite rough,' he admitted. 'But three weeks on the trail has left me in sore need of a bath and a change of clothes.'

'It was more the fact that you're a gunfighter that bothers me,' she said bluntly.

Jed silently chided himself for not having taken off

his six-gun, especially given the trouble he had just had in the saloon because of it. 'I'm no gunfighter,' he assured her. 'Actually, I'm a sheriff who's handed in his badge so I could head to Wyoming to help my uncle run his ranch.'

'Well now, why didn't you say so from the get go, young feller? It would have saved us a whole heap of ballyhoo.' She opened the door wide to him. 'You'd best come in and I'll see if I can fix you up.'

Jed stepped across the threshold clutching his carpetbag and waited while the old girl closed the door behind him.

'You'll be wanting a bath, I'll be betting. You're near covered in dust from head to foot.'

'That would be good.'

'I'll give your clothes a seeing to as well if you've got a spare set to climb into after you've had your bath.'

'That would be most kind.'

'Kindness has got nothing to do with it, young feller. I'll be charging for both the bath and washing your duds. And it's a dollar a day for your food and lodging.'

'That sounds more than fair.'

'Follow me.' Shuffling towards the long spiral staircase she painstakingly attacked the treads one at a time with either a grunt or gentle groan as she heaved her ancient body up each one until they had reached a landing. 'I'll give you the room down the end,' she said, wheezing as she waited to catch her breath back. 'It's smaller than the other rooms but it's warmer on account of catching the morning sun. The bed in there's softer too. You'll sleep the sleep of a newborn

17

babe, I can assure you of that.'

'Sounds like it's just what I'm looking for.'

Stopping, she turned around and peered at him through the gloomy light of the landing. 'How long did you say you were staying for?'

'I didn't,' he confessed. 'And I have to admit I'm not rightly sure at this stage.'

'Well, no matter. I don't often get anyone staying in that room so I figure you can have it for as long as you want.' Turning back she continued her labored walk to the room at the end of the landing.

Jed could see the old girl hadn't lied about the room. It was indeed warm, courtesy of the sun that shone brightly through the big window facing the street. 'This'll do me just fine,' he said, walking over to the window and looking down at the lively goings on in the street below.

'If you have to smoke I'd appreciate it if you'd open the window and sit close to it,' she said. 'I never could abide the smell of stale tobacco. It clings to the curtains and most everything else in a room besides. Isn't fair on the next person who has to sleep in here I reckon.'

'I'll save my smoking for when I'm outside, ma'am,' he promised.

'I think we'll get on just fine then, just so long as you drop this ma'am nonsense and call me Grandma Alice like everyone else in Paradise does.'

He grinned at her. 'You're far too young and pretty to be called grandma.'

'Get away with you,' she tittered. 'I'm about as old as

the hills, and you know it.'

'Ah, but beauty is in the eye of the beholder, Alice.'

'I don't reckon anyone is going to be seeing a beauty when they behold me . . . what did you say your name was?'

'Jed.'

'I reckon you've got yourself a way with the ladies and no mistake. Yep, a silvery tongue if ever I've come across one.'

'For all the good it's ever done me.' His mind slipped back to Belinda again. He had plied her with compliments straight from the heart, but she had still left him for another man. Sweet talk he had found would only get a man so far before it began to fail him.

Grandma Alice made for the door. 'I'll leave you to get settled in while I draw you a hot bath downstairs. I'll give you a holler when it's ready.'

Tossing his carpetbag on a chair, Jed flopped down on the bed and sighed. He couldn't remember the last time he had slept on a real feather-down mattress, and this one was everything Grandma Alice said it would be, just as soft as they came. He wouldn't have any trouble drifting off to sleep with this beneath him.

Jed spared a thought for his Uncle Tom. He would send a wire to him this afternoon and let him know he had made it as far as Paradise and was resting up here for a while before continuing on. Tom wouldn't mind him getting to the ranch a few days later than originally anticipated. He was the salt of the earth, was Jed's father's brother. Jed had the happiest memories of him from his childhood. He had been more of a father to him than an uncle. A gentle giant of a man who had taught Jed to respect the lives of men and animals alike, and never to let his temper cause him to do something he might live to regret. He was glad to say that so far he had lived up to his uncle's ideals, and looked forward to working side by side with him on his Wyoming ranch.

That evening after he had enjoyed a leisurely bath, had a shave, and a clean change of clothes, Jed lay back on that bed silently giving thanks that he had stumbled upon the township of Paradise. It would indeed be a pleasant stopover on the long and arduous journey to his new Wyoming home.

Stepping out of the door of the mercantile Jed Grayson slipped the freshly bought tobacco into his shirt pocket for safe keeping as he considered where to head to next. The café he had eaten at yesterday seemed to be calling to him from further up the street, not just the fine food but the pretty young woman who had served it to him spurred him into making an impromptu visit. However, he would call into the livery stables on his way there, to check up on his gelding and make sure he was getting the care he needed. It was important he recovered some condition if he were to carry Jed the rest of the way to Wyoming.

'Anybody there?' Jed called out as he poked his head through the double doors of the livery and squinted into the darkened interior.

There was no answer. The livery man must have stepped out for a moment, so slipping inside Jed made his way over to the stall where his gelding was happily pulling out wisps of hay from a rack.

'Is he looking after you, boy?' he murmured to the big horse. Running his hand down the animal's sleek neck then across his broad back, Jed was gratified to see the gelding was indeed being well cared for.

He didn't look around when he heard the padding of boots coming across the floor towards him from behind. 'You're doing for him just fine. He seems to be more than content,' he said, assuming it was the livery man returned from wherever he had disappeared to.

Jed Grayson felt a wracking pain suddenly grip the back of his head that drove him to his knees.

'Get his gun, Hank.'

Jed made a half-hearted grab for the Colt but his hand was brushed aside a split second before the weapon was slid free of its holster.

'Get him on his feet,' the same voice said.

Several hands were roughly grabbing him under the arms, and within seconds he was being held upright despite the protests of his wobbling legs and throbbing head.

'You honestly didn't think I'd let you get away with what you did to me yesterday, did you?'

The voice was closer now, although Jed's eyes were having trouble putting a face to it in the gloom of the stable.

'You might be fast with that gun, but you ain't got it anymore, so now you're gunna learn a lesson you ain't never gunna forget.'

Jed's head was clearing a little now; at least enough for him to make out a gloating face not more than four feet away from his. He should have guessed . . . it was the Bassett kid from his altercation in the Golden Nugget yesterday. He had obviously spotted Jed going into the stables, and seizing the opportunity for revenge, had snuck up on him. With both his arms well and truly pinioned by Bassett's lackeys, Jed was completely at his mercy.

'You tried to make me look bad in front of the men of Paradise yesterday,' Bassett said with murder in his voice.

'I didn't just try . . . I succeeded,' Jed said unwisely.

A balled-up fist hit him just below the ribcage knocking the wind out of him and radiating waves of pain throughout his belly. Jed just knew this wasn't going to go well for him.

'We don't like drifters like you coming into Paradise and throwing their weight around.' Another fist hit him in the same spot, only harder this time, so hard that Jed couldn't answer even if he had wanted to.

'I reckon his teeth'll rattle just as much as any other feller's, Zach,' a voice coming from one of the men who securely held his arms said.

'Let's find out shall we?'

Jed took a crunching blow to his jaw.

'Yep, I fancy I heard 'em rattle then,' Zach said gleefully. 'How about we rattle 'em some more?'

Blow after blow rained down on Jed's unprotected face until his eyelids were so puffed up he could barely see, and his ears so blocked up he could hardly hear.

'Work 'is ribs some more, Zach,' another voice urged.

Zach didn't need telling twice, his fists were scrunched up balls of fury that hammered Jed's ribcage from every conceivable angle until he longed for them to release their hold on him so he could slump down into the straw of the livery stables and die unmolested.

The beating continued a few minutes longer, and just when Jed thought he would die on his feet, Bassett gave his friends the order to free him. Without the support that had held him upright Jed Grayson crashed face first into the straw at Zach Bassett's feet.

'Lesson learned, I think,' the young man said self-importantly. 'But just to make sure I'll leave you with this.' A well heeled boot lashed out and caught Jed in the ribs as he foolishly tried to get to his hands and knees, forcing him prostrate once again.

'You get yourself out of town as soon as you can climb on that gelding of yours,' Bassett said menacingly. 'If I see you in Paradise after tomorrow I'll make you wish you'd never heard the name Zachary Bassett.'

Jed didn't know how long he lay there after they had left the livery stables. It could have been half an hour, or it could have been more. Eventually the thought came to him that he would have to seek help or he wasn't going to make it through to the morning, so drawing on what little strength he had left he hauled himself to his trembling legs and staggered out the door on to the street. He hadn't gone more than thirty yards when feminine hands were clutching at his shirt in an effort to keep him on his feet, and although the kind soul attempting to help him was saying something to him, his damaged eardrum failed to decipher it. Several yards on and everything went black, and Jedidiah Heath Grayson fell in an unconscious heap in the dust of Paradise's main street.

CHAPTER THREE

Jed opened first one puffy eyelid and then the other, and instantly wished he hadn't. The light streaming in from the chink in the curtains was falling directly on his face, and it made his injured eyes sting with the pain it caused.

'So you're finally awake.' Grandma Alice got out of the rocker beside Jed's bed and peered down at him. 'They really worked you over, and some more to boot,' she said sympathetically.

Jed was aware enough of his surroundings to figure out he was in the small room he had rented off Alice. 'How did I get here?' he managed to rasp out from the depths of his sore, dry throat.

'You were found in the street by a young woman. She got a few of the men of the town to carry you up here. It was no easy task, I can tell you. You're a big feller and those stairs are steep. Those poor men were in a sorry state by the time they got you into that bed you're lying in now.'

Jed's mind wandered back. 'There was a gal. . . .'

'Laney Landers,' Grandma Alice said, anticipating his question. 'She's a pretty gal that works at the Silver Dollar Saloon down the far end of town. Sings and dances and generally entertains the customers.'

He made a mental note to go and thank the woman just as soon as he was up on his feet again. 'How long have I. . . ?'

Grandma Alice beat him to the punch again. 'You've been out cold for three days.'

Three days. Jed had no recollection of anything from the moment he collapsed out on the street until he had come to a few minutes back. The beating he took in the livery stables came flooding back to him though, a more savage beating he had never taken in his life, nor did he wish to ever again.

'Any idea who did this to you?'

'The Bassett kid.'

'Zach Bassett? Now why doesn't that surprise me?' She looked down at him in a motherly fashion. 'I figure he and his pals jumped you from behind. You seem to me the type of feller that would be more than a match for Zach if it had been a fair fight.'

'They jumped me,' Jed confirmed.

'It's long since time something was done about that boy. His father lets him run riot in this county and nobody is safe from him, either male or female.'

'The sheriff. . . ?'

'John Tanner? Why, he's as good as in Jason Bassett's back pocket. He pulls Tanner out and dusts him off every time he needs the law to back him up. Even if you were to go to Tanner with eyewitnesses to what that boy

26

did, you wouldn't get any joy out of Sheriff John Tanner. Nope, he's well and truly Jason Bassett's man, and that's the way he'll stay, no matter what.'

Jed thought over what Alice had just told him. His first thought had been to go to the law and leave it up to them to bring young Zachary Bassett to justice for the savage attack on his person. But if what the old lady had just told him was true, then it could backfire on him in spectacular fashion. So if anything was to be done about it, and Jed was determined something should be, then he was going to have to do it himself just as soon as he was well enough to.

Grandma Alice made a move towards the door. 'I'll leave you to wake up properly without me bothering you. There's a jug of water and a glass on the table beside your bed. You'll be a mite parched by now I should think, seeing it's been three days since you last had a drink.'

'Thanks, Alice.'

'Ring that little bell beside the jug if you need me, and I'll come running!' She chuckled then. 'Though it'll be more like a slow shuffle I reckon, given my age, but I'll get to you in the end.'

Jed considered the situation he found himself in now. Heading for Wyoming was out of the question for the time being. In fact, he wouldn't be up and walking, let alone riding a horse, for another four or five days. He would have to get Alice to send a wire to his uncle and let him know of the delay so he wouldn't worry when Jed didn't turn up on time.

He would have to get some more money to the livery

27

stable man, too. Jed's gelding was going to be lodging with that feller for much longer than had first been anticipated. But what really occupied his mind at the moment was how he was going to deal with the problem of Zachary Bassett, because there was no way he was going to leave Paradise before he had taught the youngster that what he had done to Jed Grayson was going to cost him dearly.

Jed didn't recognize the pretty face that peered around the door of his bedroom the next day and smiled at him. 'Grandma Alice told me to come right on up,' the owner of that pretty face said. 'I'm right glad you're feeling better.'

Jed was suddenly even more aware of his aching ribs and swollen face than he had been previously. 'If this is feeling better, then I'd hate to remember how I felt before,' he quipped. The smile on the young beauty's face deepened as she left the cover of the door and entered the room, giving him his first unimpeded view of her.

She was tall for a woman, all of five feet nine inches Jed figured, and she had a figure to match the beautiful face. Long legs attached to a wide set of hips, a narrow waist and full breasts was a combination that was enough to get any man's pulse racing, even one as broken up as Jed was at the moment. The long wavy black hair she wore down cascaded over her shoulders and halfway down her back, adding to her appeal. Yep, whoever she was she could hold her own against any woman and come out on top in the attractiveness stakes.

'I guess you'll be wondering who I am,' she said as she sat down in Grandma Alice's rocker and fixed her green eyes on his sky-blue ones.

'I thought for a moment I had died and gone to heaven and you were one of God's angels,' he joked.

The smile on her face broadened, which only served to make her even more appealing than ever. 'Not quite.' She held out her hand. 'I'm Laney Landers.'

The name struck a chord. 'You're the kind woman who helped me out on the street. I owe you a debt of gratitude for that.'

'If I hadn't done it someone else would have come along soon enough and helped you out,' she said humbly.

'But it wasn't someone else, it was you,' he pointed out.

'Well, at any rate I'm glad you've pulled through. There was a time there when I began to doubt you were going to make it.'

It suddenly dawned on him that she had been visiting him while he had been unconscious. 'Alice didn't tell me I'd had visitors while I was out cold.'

'Didn't she?'

He shook his head.

'I would come in here and sit in this very chair and just watch you breathing and pray you would come out of it all right,' she confessed. 'And here you are, and you seem to be on the mend.'

'I am on the mend,' he said, more to put her mind at rest than anything else, because he knew he had a long way to go yet before he was going to be up and around.

'Grandma Alice told me it was Zach Bassett and his friends that did this to you.'

'Yep, and they did a mighty fine job of it too. No stone left unturned, so to speak.'

'I don't know how you can joke about it. I'd be screaming blue murder if they'd done it to me.'

'There's not much else I can do, laid up like this.' He tried to raise his head a little so he could see her face better but the effort was too much for him, and he was forced to slump back into the pillow.

Witnessing his failure she got out of the rocker, then slipping one hand behind his head and lifting it, deftly pulled another pillow across to prop behind his neck, before gently releasing her hold.

'That's much better, thank you,' he said sincerely.

'My pleasure.'

'Now that I'm no longer in the land of nod, does that mean your visits are going to stop?'

She smiled sweetly at him. 'Not if you don't want them to.'

'I don't want them to,' he said quickly.

'Then they won't stop.'

He was pleased. He wasn't too sure why. He hadn't really got over what Belinda had done to him, yet here he was hoping against hope that a woman he had only just met would make him the promise that she would come and see him again. He must be out of his mind. The physical pain he was feeling now was nothing compared to the mental anguish Belinda Carrington had put him through. And yet there was something about this young beauty that told him she was different. Her easy style of conversation that marked her out as humble despite her good looks, and the disarming smile that put him at his ease, seemed to break down all his defences.

'I should leave now and let you sleep,' she said, taking the pause in the conversation to mean he was tired.

He reached out his hand and gently grabbed her wrist as she turned to go. 'No, please don't go yet.'

She looked down at his big tanned hand enclosed around her pale wrist, and then looked into his eyes. 'I don't want to outstay my welcome.'

He made sure his eyes never left hers for so much as a second. 'You couldn't if you tried.'

He thought she looked pleased, but couldn't tell for sure. Letting go of his grip on her he was relieved when she sat back down in Grandma Alice's rocker.

'You have a family?' he asked, more to discover if she was married than anything else.

'My parents died when I was fourteen and my older sister of scarlet fever not long after she and I arrived in Paradise. That was about eight years ago. I was eighteen at the time. If it hadn't been for Floyd I think I would have starved. I was a real greenhorn back then.'

His heart sank. So there was a man in her life after all. He had been foolish to hope there wouldn't be. Especially given the fact she was so beautiful.

'Floyd took me in and fed and clothed me until I was able to repay him,' she continued.

That didn't sound good. Just what was this 'Floyd' fellow expecting her to do for him?

31

'I dance and sing at his saloon,' she explained, as if she could read his thoughts. 'I guess you could say he's been like a father to me these past eight years. I haven't found a man I wanted courting me, so I haven't started a family of my own yet. Maybe I never will.'

Relief flooded over Jed in a massive wave. There was nothing going on between the two of them. Floyd was merely a kindly older man who had given a young girl a home and job when she was down and almost out. He knew it was crazy, but he couldn't have been happier at the revelation.

'I will have to come and hear you sing when I am on my feet again.'

'I doubt you'd find it entertaining.'

'If your voice matches your stunning face then I'm sure you must sing like one of the angels.'

She blushed, and to try and hide her discomfort she placed her hand in front of her rapidly reddening face.

He instantly regretted the comment. 'I'm sorry; I've made you feel uncomfortable.'

'I don't know why I'm reacting like this,' she confessed sheepishly. 'Men pay me compliments like that all the time and I hardly raise an eyebrow. I don't know why it should be any different this time.'

'Maybe it's because I'm so rakishly good-looking,' he said grinning at her, attempting to diffuse the situation with a little humour, and it seemed to work because the hand came away from the face as she giggled at his silly comment.

'As it is you are rather handsome.'

He laughed. 'I need to get myself beat up more

often. I don't think anyone's ever said that to me before, not even Belinda.'

Now it was her turn to look worried, and he noticed it straightaway. 'Belinda was a woman I thought I was going to marry once,' he put in quickly so as not to ruin the way things had been going between the two of them so far, 'but she decided she liked a certain gambler more and took up with him instead.'

The worried look was replaced with a smile. 'That was her loss.'

'I am definitely going to have to keep you around; you are good for my ego.'

'I really ought to be going,' she said, rising from the rocker and smoothing her dress out as she did so. 'I need to get ready for the midday show down at the Silver Dollar. But I'll come back and see how you are tomorrow if you like.'

'I would like that very much.'

'Same time tomorrow then,' she said and then headed for the door.

'Laney . . .' he called after her.

She stopped in the doorway and turned around to look at him.

'Thank you for coming to see me.'

She smiled one of those fabulous smiles again, and then was gone before he had time to say anything else, her shoes tapping out a melody on the ancient wooden treads of the stairway, as she descended hastily towards the ground floor of Grandma Alice's boarding house.

Jed let his head sink deep into the plumped-up pillow and released a little sigh. He had originally planned to get himself better and then square things with the Bassett kid before leaving the township of Paradise behind forever, but he had a strange feeling that those plans were about to change, and that had everything to do with a green-eyed beauty who went by the name of Laney Landers.

CHAPTER FOUR

'It does my poor old heart good to see you up and around at last,' Grandma Alice said as Jed joined her at the breakfast table a week after he had come round from the attack. 'I was worried you weren't ever going to be able to walk again after the beating you took.'

'I had a few fears along those lines myself, Alice,' Jed admitted. 'But you know what they say about not being able to keep a good man down!'

She chuckled at his comment. 'I wonder what fool dreamed that one up. I've seen many a good man down for the count in my eighty-two years on this earth.' Grasping the coffee pot in her shaky hands she tilted it up and poured its contents into a china cup, then offered the drink to him.

'Thanks.' Picking up the brimming cup, he held it between his palms and felt the hot liquid radiate its warmth deep into his hands. 'I might venture outside today.'

She looked at him with concern in her aged eyes.

'Do you think that's wise? What if you run into the Bassett boy?'

'I'll wish him all the best and invite him to join me in a drink down at the Golden Nugget.'

The comment threw her for a moment until she saw the flicker of a smile dance across his lips. 'By jingo you remind me of my Harry,' she said wistfully. 'He had a sense of humour like yours, God rest his soul. I think that's what I miss the most about him. He always could make me laugh when I was feeling down.'

'I'll be on the lookout for Zach Bassett, don't you worry about that, Alice,' Jed said in a more serious manner. 'I won't get caught out by him again, I can assure you of that.'

'I hope not, 'cos I've come to be rather fond of you, Jed Grayson, and so has a much younger woman whose name shall remain unspoken.'

She was referring to Laney Landers, of course, and the unexpected comment brought a great deal of plea-sure to Jed. He had grown very fond of Laney himself this past week, and had looked forward to her daily visits to his little room at the far end of the landing with relish – though perhaps with him being better those visits would now stop. He hoped not.

'I don't think I've ever seen a gal so love-struck as that one is over you,' Alice continued. 'She fair floats down those stairs after a visit with you. I swear she's on cloud nine when she leaves this house.'

Jed was pleased to hear that. He had sworn off women after Belinda, but Laney had come along and changed his mind for him. He would be over the moon if what Alice was saying turned out to be true.

'This town could live up to its name if it weren't for the Bassett family,' Alice said sadly. 'Take them out of the picture and this town'd be the perfect place for a man to settle down and raise a family.'

Jed peered at Grandma Alice over the top of his coffee cup. 'Sounds as if you've got me married off to Laney already.'

'And why not? She's a lovely gal, and anyone can see you need a good woman to take care of you. You couldn't do better than Laney Landers, Jed, I'll tell you that for nothing!'

Placing the cup down on the table Jed placed his hands in the air in an admission of defeat. 'All right . . . all right . . . I give up. She's a good woman and she'd make a fine wife.'

'You just make sure you don't let her slip through your fingers, then.'

'I'll do my best.'

'You'd better, or you'll have me to answer to.'

After breakfast Jed left the house with trepidation. He still wasn't back to his best yet, that would take another couple of weeks at least, but with his Navy Colt on his hip he was determined he wouldn't be taking any nonsense from Zachary Bassett or his sidekicks should he run across them.

As Jed parted the batwings at the Golden Nugget Saloon his eyes made a quick sweep of the smoky interior to make sure trouble wasn't lurking in one of its dark corners before making his way over to the bar.

The bartender who had served him that first day he

rode into town looked at him as if he was seeing a ghost.
'I heard you were beaten to within an inch of your life
and then run out of town,' he said, the surprise in his
brown eyes betraying the fact he couldn't quite believe
that what he saw standing in front of him was quite real.

'A story circulated by Zachary Bassett no doubt?'

'Yes, it was Zach I heard it from,' the bartender
admitted. 'The way he told it you were as good as dead.'

'Well, as you can see I'm very much alive,' Jed said,
plonking some coins down on the counter. 'Give me a
bottle of that good whiskey you gave me last time.'

'Sure.' The man twisted round, and reaching up
above the big mirror behind the bar, pulled a bottle
down from the top shelf.

Jed waited for him to produce a glass before uncork-
ing the bottle and tipping a generous amount of the
dark liquid into it. 'I've earned this,' he said before
tossing that dark liquid down his throat in one swift
movement.

'Barely touched the sides,' the bartender said in
admiration.

'That was the warm-up glass. The second one will
definitely make contact,' Jed promised.

'So what did happen between you and Zach?' the
bartender asked after Jed had downed his second
whiskey.

Their eyes locked. 'Zachary Bassett would have to be
the biggest coward I've ever run across in my entire life,
and that's really saying something because I've met
some cowards in my time.'

The entire bar had gone quiet when Jed had walked

in, and now they listened intently to the conversation between the two men with interest, only an occasional hushed whisper breaking the silence.

'So it wasn't a fair fight?'

'Does Bassett even know what that means?'

'He's been telling everyone this past week that it was. Said you were no good without your gun. Said you barely touched him with your fists before you went down.'

'He got that last bit right I suppose,' Jed said scornfully. 'The fact is I didn't lay a hand on him. It's kinda hard to do that when you get hit from behind and then two men hold you while Bassett beats up on you.'

A murmur of excited voices did the rounds of the Golden Nugget Saloon. This was news to them. All week long Zach Bassett had been bragging on how he had kicked the butt of Thomas Thornton's hired gunman and then kicked him out of town. But not a man in that saloon had any trouble believing that the story the man standing at the bar right now was telling was the true version.

'He'll sure be surprised when he comes into town next and sees you still here,' the bartender said.

'He's gunna be a whole heap more than just surprised, I can promise you,' Jed said with passion in his voice.

'You intendin' to be gunning for him?'

'Maybe . . . it'll depend on how he reacts.'

'How he reacts to what?'

'To me kicking him around out on the street like the dog that he is.'

'That's gunna be easier said than done, mister. Zach surrounds himself with hands from his father's ranch that protect him. You'd have to go through them first to get to him.'

'Zachary Bassett's no good friends don't scare me. I'm willing to bet they'll turn tail and run if they think their lives are at risk.'

'So there's gunna be some lead flying after all?'

Jed swallowed another glass of the top shelf whiskey. 'Hang around and find out.' Pushing the bottle back across the counter, Jed turned to go. 'Save what's left in that bottle for me, will you,' he said over his shoulder. 'I'll be back to celebrate when the job's done.'

Jed was no more than ten yards clear of the saloon when he heard the batwings swish backwards and forwards causing his hand to go immediately to the butt of his Navy Colt in anticipation.

'I'm not looking for trouble,' the voice behind him hastened to say, 'I just want to speak to you for a moment.'

Jed turned around to see a slender man in plaid shirt and leather chaps step down off the boardwalk and make his way towards him.

'Speak to me about what exactly?' Jed asked guardedly.

The man held out his hand in greeting but Jed just stood there regarding him coolly.

The man withdrew the proffered hand. 'Well, this ain't off to a good start.'

'State your business,' Jed said bluntly.

'I'm Jack Wilson, the foreman for the Circle D

Ranch. That's Thomas Thornton's spread.'

'I've heard of the man,' Jed said, his demeanour not softening any at the revelation the man standing in front of him worked for the arch enemy of the Bassett family.

'The truth is. . . ?' Wilson searched for the name.

Jed obliged him. 'It's Grayson.'

'The truth is, Mr Grayson, that my boss is looking for a man like you to protect his interests from the Bassetts.'

'A man like me. . . ?'

'A man who can handle a gun,' Wilson explained. 'I can't help noticing how you wear yours. I figure you can handle it pretty good.'

'I'm no hired gun,' Jed said as he turned to go.

Jack Wilson's hand shot out and grabbed Jed by the arm to stop him from leaving before he had heard him out.

'I think you'd better take your hand off me if you know what's good for you,' Jed said in a low menacing voice.

'I'm sorry,' Wilson apologized. 'I didn't mean any disrespect by it. It's just that Mr Thornton and me . . . well, we're getting kinda desperate, and when I heard you'd had a run-in with Zach Bassett and I saw that gun you wear I figured you might just be the answer to our prayers.'

'Well I ain't,' Jed said bluntly. He turned to leave again.

'Mr Thornton would pay you well,' Wilson called after him. 'He's a more than generous man. What you would make from this would give you the deposit on a little spread of your own, if you're interested.'

'I ain't.'

Jack Wilson sighed. He had hoped against hope that this tall, handsome stranger was going to be their saviour where the Bassett family was concerned, but evidently he had been wrong. It seemed they were going to have to tackle the threat from Jason Bassett themselves without the help of a seasoned gunfighter.

CHAPTER FIVE

Jed Grayson sat on the edge of his bed in Grandma Alice's boarding house and counted out his money. 'Five dollars and forty cents,' he muttered despondently to himself. He was going to have to find some work and real soon, or his stay in this establishment would soon be over. The thing being, he had scraped up just enough money to get him to his uncle's ranch in Wyoming. He had never figured he would be laid up in a town he had never even heard of before the day he first laid eyes on it. But laid up he had been, for over two weeks now, and that had seriously depleted his resources.

Most of the cuts and bruises had healed now, although his ribs were a bit sore here and there. He wondered what sort of work he could pick up to tide himself over until he was recovered enough to climb back up into the saddle and head off on that arduous ride to Wyoming. A bit of carpentry work maybe? He always had been pretty handy with a hammer and saw. Mending chairs, tables, wagons, even helping with building houses sometimes. Yep, he could turn his hand to most anything in the woodwork line of things. He would ask Charlie the bartender down at the Golden Nugget if he knew of anything going. He seemed to be a feller in the know about most things.

'Try Sam Judson the wheelwright,' Charlie had suggested when Jed had asked him about it later on that day. 'He was only saying to me last week that he had more work than he could handle.'

'Where would I find this Judson feller?'

'Right down the far end of town, just before that two-storey house with the poison ivy climbing up the walls.'

'I know the house. Thanks, Charlie, I owe you one,' he turned to go.

'Jed . . .'

He turned back, 'Yep?'

'I hear tell Zach Bassett's heard you're still in town.'

'It was only a matter of time before he did,' Jed said philosophically.

'He's saying he's gunna finish the job he started. He's just crazy enough to try it, too. So you be careful walking around out there where he can see you.'

'I'll be ready for him this time, Charlie, don't you worry about that. I've never been caught out by the same feller twice, and I don't aim to start now.'

Jed stuck to the cover of the boardwalk roof so he wouldn't be easily seen as he made his way down towards the far end of town. He wasn't scared of Bassett, but he wasn't going to go courting trouble either, not just now at least anyway. Nope, he would pick a time of his own choosing when he settled up with young

Zachary Bassett, and when he did, the fellow would end up wishing he had never heard the name Jed Grayson.

'Sam Judson?' he asked, when he had reached the wheelwright's shop and come across a man labouring away at a wagon wheel beneath the light of an open window.

'You're speaking to him,' the man said as he straightened up from his work and cast his eye over the stranger.

'I heard from Charlie Watson down at the Golden Nugget that you might be interested in taking a man on for a week or two until you've got through your backlog of work.'

Judson's eyes were on Jed's low-slung gun. 'You wouldn't happen to be that gunfighter that Zach Bassett and his pals took to a couple of weeks back, would you?'

'I'm not a gunfighter,' Jed corrected him. 'I was a sheriff once, but that was a good while ago now.'

'Gunfighter, sheriff, they're pretty much the same thing in a lawless town, aren't they?'

Jed could sense the opportunity to find work beginning to slip away from him. 'Some folks might see it that way, I suppose.'

'But not you?'

'I've always stayed on the right side of the law. If there's no work for me here then I'll just go and let you get on with it.' He turned and began to retrace his footsteps back toward the saloon.

'Now, just wait on a minute there,' Judson said quickly. 'I never said there wasn't any work for you.'

Halting his retreat from the shop Jed looked back at the man. 'I figured the questions you were asking me were intended to let me know you didn't think highly enough of me to take me on.'

'I like to gauge a feller's intentions before I go offering him anything,' Judson said, leaning the almost finished wheel against the wall and moving over to where Jed was standing by the door. 'Can't have a feller here who attracts trouble for me. You ain't planning on doing that, by any chance, are you?'

Jed shook his head. 'All I want is to make enough money to get myself to Wyoming. I've got an uncle down that way who wants me to help him run his ranch.'

'That's good honest work.' He looked at Jed thoughtfully for a moment. 'You got any experience at this kinda work?'

'I've turned my hand to it in the past.'

Judson rubbed the stubble on his chin with the palm of his right hand as he thought the whole thing over. 'I'll tell you what,' he said eventually. 'I need the fellies over there,' he pointed to a jumble of wooden arches lying in the corner, 'mortised and joined together. Spokes need putting in too. If you do a good enough job of that I'll take you on for a couple of weeks.'

Slipping his jacket off, Jed tossed it across a barrel and began rolling up the sleeves of his shirt. 'I'll get onto it right away.'

'I'm making it for old man Travis' buckboard. Promised him I'd have it finished by tonight, but there's no way I'm gunna be able to keep that promise without help.'

'Leave it to me,' Jed said with quiet resolve. 'I'll make sure Mr Travis has his wagon wheel finished and fitted before we close up the shop tonight.'

Jed was as good as his word. The spokes were tightly fitted and the fellies joined before the sun had begun to sink over the horizon. Old man Travis arrived just as Jed had finished fitting the wheel to his buckboard.

'Well now, that's jist fine,' he said as he looked the new wheel over. 'Shame the rest of the wagon isn't in such fine fettle.'

'I'm glad you're happy with it, Mr Travis,' Jed said, pleased that his labours hadn't gone unnoticed.

'You're that feller that the young Bassett boy beat up on, ain't you?' the old man asked when he had straightened up from inspecting the wheel.

'So every man and his dog keep on reminding me,' Jed said morosely.

Travis chuckled. 'There ain't no shame in taking a beating when you're outnumbered, lad, and from what I heard you were jumped from behind as well.'

Jed looked at him in surprise. He hadn't known that Zach Bassett's cowardly attack had become common knowledge. Maybe the men in the Golden Nugget who had overheard his conversation with the bartender had spread the word.

The old fellow picked up on his surprise. 'The Landers woman told me about it,' he explained. 'I've just come from the Silver Dollar. Dang, that little gal can sing. A man don't want for entertainment when she gets to airin' her lungs.'

Jed suddenly realized he hadn't had that particular pleasure yet. He really must go and catch one of her shows real soon.

After Travis had taken his buckboard Sam Judson walked over to where Jed was watching the wagon disappear down the street and extended his hand. 'As far as I'm concerned you're the man for the job,' he said amiably.

Jed took the proffered hand and shook it firmly. 'Thank you, Mr Judson, I won't let you down.'

'Call me "Sam", that'll do just fine,' he said with a smile hovering around his lips. ' "Mr Judson" just makes me sound too dang old.'

' "Sam" it is, then.'

'You get yourself on home or down to the saloon for a drink, if that's your thing,' Sam said. He looked up at the rapidly sinking sun. 'I reckon this working day has come to an end.'

Jed nodded, 'Same time tomorrow then?'

'Yep, we've got a stack of spokes to make and a few hubs to fashion as well. It'll be a busy day, that's for sure.'

'I look forward to it,' Jed said sincerely. It had felt good using his hands to make something useful for a change.

Jed decided to give the saloon a miss and head for Grandma Alice's for a warm bath and a hot meal. It had been a long, tiring day and he fancied a quiet evening in his room reading the newspaper. He was trudging along the street towards the boarding house when he spotted none other than Zachary Bassett gazing into the front window of the mercantile at a new Winchester rifle on display. He had his back to Jed, and what was more, he was alone.

Tiptoeing across the street Jed carefully stepped up on to the boardwalk in front of the mercantile and reaching over, quickly slipped the young man's six-gun clear out of his holster.

'Hey, what's the big idea?' Bassett bellowed as he spun around to see who was playing a prank on him. Then he saw who it was, and his face went deathly pale.

Jed tossed the six-gun out on to the street where Bassett couldn't get his hands on it. 'I'm back for round two,' he said coldly. 'But this time it's gunna be one on one. No more of this three against one malarkey.'

Jed grinned as Zachary Bassett's eyes desperately combed both sides of the street. 'Your pals can't help you this time.' Taking off his jacket he tossed it over the hitching rail in the street below him. 'You made a big mistake when you hit me from behind and did what you did to me, 'cos I'm not a man to ever let something like that go. Now you're gunna get back as good as you gave me, but I doubt you're gunna be man enough to handle it.'

Zachary Bassett had mercilessly beaten Jed Grayson that day in the livery. If Grayson was any sort of ordinary man he would want revenge. He knew he was no match for Grayson without his friends around to swing the contest in his favour. 'My pa will have your guts for garters,' he said frantically as Jed finished up sorting out his shirt sleeves and raised his fists ready for business.

'Maybe so, but before that happens your pa is gunna get you back in tiny little pieces.'

Bassett backed away from the advancing ex-sheriff. 'You stay away from me,' he demanded shakily.

'Not a chance. You've got this coming to you, boy!'

Jed threw out a left jab that hit Bassett flush in the mouth, instantly splitting his top lip and sending a trickle of warm blood down his chin.

Fear came into the youngster's eyes. He hadn't forgotten the savagery of his attack in the livery stables that night not more than two weeks ago, and he had genuinely believed that the results of it would be the end of the matter between him and the man who went by the name of Jed Grayson. So to see him now, standing in front of him, full of malice and a grim determination to pay back the wrong done to him, filled Zach Bassett with dread.

'I have never thought much of a man who hides behind others,' Jed said, as his second jab landed squarely on the bridge of Bassett's nose, mashing it sideways. 'There's something decidedly unmanly about doing that.'

A throbbing pain gripped Zach's busted snout, and it was all he could do to stop himself from screaming out in agony.

'You see, your pa's made a grave mistake giving you free rein to do whatever you want. You simply ain't man enough to use that freedom wisely.' He drove a right fist under Bassett's ribcage, forcing the boy to double up as he tried to suck in enough air to keep his lungs working.

Zach Bassett had enough presence of mind to realize if he didn't do something, and do it quick, then he was going to end up a broken and bleeding mess. Mustering what strength he had, he launched himself at Jed with a wild swinging of his arms hoping to land a punch that would put Jed Grayson down on the boardwalk.

Jed ducked, dived, weaved and swayed. Not a single punch from the young man paid dividends: he was simply completely outclassed by the older man.

Jed threw a left hook, followed closely by a right cross that punished Bassett's brittle jaw. Vigorously tossing his head side to side to prevent himself from slipping into unconsciousness, Jason Bassett's son struggled to maintain his footing. If he went down he would be completely at the mercy of the man to whom he had shown absolutely none, and that would produce some disastrous results.

'You know what's gunna happen to you if you go down, don't you?' Jed said, as if he knew what Bassett had just been thinking. He hit him with a sudden flurry of shots that connected on various parts of his body. 'I figure after this your face ain't ever gunna look the same again.'

Zach Bassett tried to stagger off down the boardwalk in a vain attempt to escape his fate, but Jed was on to him in a jiffy, 'Oh no you don't!' Seizing him by the collar he swung him full force into the pole holding the boardwalk roof up, the crunching blow jarring every bone in the young man's torso. 'We're not finished until I say so.'

Zach feared for his life now. Grayson was obviously

intent on completely destroying him. If he didn't get away soon he was certain he would die in a pool of his own blood right there in front of the mercantile store display window.

Holding on to the pole Bassett summoned what little was left of his strength and swung himself down on to the street. Landing with a thump on his hands and knees he immediately picked himself up, and with a will born of desperation he began a stumbling run towards the safety of the Golden Nugget Saloon.

Stepping lithely off the boardwalk Jed trotted after him. 'It's not over until you can no longer stand, Bassett.'

Zach's heart beat faster than it ever had before. He couldn't have feared for his life any more if it had been the very devil himself after him.

Jed caught up with him just before he made it to the middle of the street. 'You didn't let me leave that day in the livery, so I don't see why I should let you.'

Zach Bassett spun round to face him. He was a cornered beast that had nowhere to hide. All he could do now was fight. With both fists swinging wildly he prayed something would connect and do the damage he needed so he could save his skin. If this failed then he was out of options.

Jed batted each and every feeble attempt away with the scorn it deserved. Zachary Bassett was spent, not that he had much to offer in the first place – he was strictly a brawler who relied on downing his opponent early on in the piece. Taken the distance, he soon succumbed to someone with superior fighting ability.

Jed decided the time had come to finish it. Landing a severe combination of head shots he stepped back long enough to watch the Bassett boy crash heavily to the ground before aiming a vicious kick into his ribcage. 'I believe that was the spot you got me,' he said without a hint of remorse.

Stepping over the unconscious man Jed headed for the saloon. 'I think this calls for a celebratory drink. There's nothing like downing a stiff whiskey after justice has been served.'

CHAPTER SIX

The dawn's grey light had only just begun to penetrate through the chinks in Jed's curtains when he was woken by the ruckus going on downstairs. He could hear Grandma Alice's strained voice shouting angrily. Propping himself up on one elbow he turned his ear towards the partially open door trying to pick up what was being said.

'You aren't coming in here,' Grandma Alice was saying insistently. 'This is my house and I'll say who crosses the threshold and who doesn't.'

'Out of my way, old woman, or I'll move you myself,' a man's irate voice thundered back.

'Over my dead body you will.'

'If that's what it takes, then so be it!'

As Grandma Alice's scream sped up the stairs to greet Jed's ears, he leapt from his bed and snatching up the shotgun he had left propped against the wall beside the door, quickly fed two shells into it and went out on to the landing to investigate.

'Get out ... get out of my house, Bassett!' Alice hollered.

Reaching the top of the stairs Jed peered cautiously down the rickety stairwell to see three men ascending – and what was more, they seemed to be in an all-fired hurry.

'Bassett, huh,' Jed mumbled to himself as he clicked the double barrel shut and trained it on the advancing men. None of them was Zach Bassett, so it had to be the old man himself.

'That's quite far enough!' Jed ordered, his finger sitting snugly on the first trigger.

Jason Bassett halted his progress and looked up the stairs in surprise. 'Are you the feller they call Grayson?' he demanded.

'What of it?'

'I'm looking for the man who savagely beat my son and left him out in the middle of the street last night. My ranch hands brought him home all busted up some time after midnight.'

'If your son is Zach Bassett then I'm the man you're looking for,' Jed said coldly. 'Last night he got a healthy dose of his own medicine.

'It was anything but healthy,' Jason Bassett roared furiously. 'A punch-up is one thing, but he was dang near dead.'

'Pretty much the state he left me in down at the livery stables a few weeks ago when he and his buddies jumped me,' Jed answered with just as much venom in his voice.

The look on the older man's face told Jed he didn't

know anything about that particular incident.

'He didn't tell you what he did to me, I take it?'

Bassett only took seconds to recover from the revelation his son had brought the beating on himself. 'I don't dang well care what he did to you,' he hissed. 'No one does what you did to a Bassett and gets away with it.'

'Well, unless you are prepared to reach for that shooting iron on your hip, I rather think I have, don't you?'

The man's face flushed red with fury. He was the king of this county, and he wasn't going to stand here and let some saddle-bum speak to him like this. He resumed his ascent of the stairs, determined to get his hands on the upstart and thrash him for all he was worth.

Jed raised the double-barrel to eye level and took aim. 'Unless you want to die on these stairs, I suggest you stop right where you are!'

Bassett's hand touched the butt of his six-gun.

'Yep, you go right on ahead and pull that iron,' Jed said calmly. 'It'd give me all the reason I need to blow you back down those stairs.'

Jason Bassett stopped on the sixth tread from the top of the landing and glared up at Jed. He could see the man meant business. He would pull that trigger if need be.

'This ain't over,' he said menacingly. 'You picked the wrong town to ride into that day you turned your horse's head in the direction of Paradise. You ain't ever gunna leave now. I'm gunna make sure you get yourself buried here, and that's gunna be a whole heap sooner than you think.'

'That's mighty big talk from a money-grubbing, back-stabbing swindler like you, Bassett. I've heard how you force the smaller ranchers off their land so you can gobble it all up for yourself. You might be good at bullying those hard-working men, but you ain't no match for a man like me.'

'A man like you . . . one who beats up on a kid you mean?'

'He's a kid who gangs up on an innocent man and does his best to break every bone in his body. That's a kid who deserves everything that's dished up to him. Stop defending the little punk and start disciplining him. He's terrorized enough folks in Paradise as it is.'

'Zach is gunna inherit everything I've fought so hard to build up these past thirty years. He'll be the biggest rancher for a hundred miles either side of Paradise. A man like that deserves to be treated with respect.'

'Respect is earned, Bassett, and neither you nor your son has earned any from anyone in this town.'

The insult stung Jason Bassett hard. He would dearly have loved to pull his Remington and sling some hot lead in the upstart's direction, but there was no way he would survive the shotgun blast he knew would come his way if he tried it. The only option left open to him was to beat a retreat down the stairs and bide his time where this man was concerned. The day would come that he would bring him to his knees and make him pay. He would beg for mercy then, but Jason Bassett was determined that none would be extended to him.

Turning abruptly he went back down the way he had come up without saying another word.

Jed nipped downstairs to check on Grandma Alice. He found her sitting on the floor, her back up against the wall beside the front door that Bassett hadn't bothered to close behind him on his way out.

'Are you all right, Alice?' he asked with concern as he leaned his shotgun against the wall and squatted down to check out her injuries.

'I'll live . . . I just need to get my breath back, is all,' she gasped in a lungful of air before continuing. 'That brute shoved me over when I told him he couldn't come inside. I reckon that, and all the shouting I did, have made it a bit hard for me to breathe.'

Helping her up, Jed guided her over to a chair.

'You'll have to find somewhere else to live now,' she said when her breathing had settled down enough for her to resume speaking normally. 'He'll come back here again during the early hours of the morning some time when we're both asleep. The first thing you'd know about it would be waking up to see a gun barrel pointing right at you.'

Jed knew Alice was right. Bassett would be back, and with more men next time. Zach Bassett had been taught his lesson, and so there was nothing to hold Jed in Paradise any longer. Maybe now was the time for him to head for Wyoming and that job waiting for him on his uncle's ranch. If he stayed, Jason Bassett would hurt anyone Jed had an attachment to, so that would put Laney squarely at risk, and that was one person he dearly wanted to protect.

'Will he hurt you when he comes back?' Jed asked, suddenly realizing he wouldn't be here to protect Alice when he did.

She shook her old head. 'It's you he wants. I'll just let him in to search the place and tell him you've gone who knows where, and I reckon he'll leave without giving me so much as a backward glance. An old woman like me holds no interest for him.'

Jed hoped she was right. He would hate to think she might get hurt because of him, and of course he would never know anything about it if he was already halfway to Wyoming when Bassett paid her that visit.

'I'll head off today, Alice. I think it'd be better all round if I did. I can't say I like doing it, it makes me feel as if I'm running from Jason Bassett, and I've never run from a fight in my life. But I don't want anyone else getting hurt on my account.'

She didn't say anything, and so he took it that she agreed with him. 'Are you all right now?' he asked gently.

'As right as rain,' she stood up and seemed to be back to her usual self. 'I'll rustle you up some breakfast.'

Jed headed back upstairs to gather up his belongings. He would eat with Alice for the last time, then swing by the Silver Dollar to say goodbye to Laney Landers, and then head on out of town before any more trouble came his way.

Tears came into Laney's eyes when he told her of his plans. 'I was hoping you might change your mind and decide to settle down here in Paradise,' she said wist-fully. 'I'm going to miss you when you're gone.'

'It's for the best, Laney. I've made enemies of the Bassett family, and that would mean someone would have to die sooner or later. I'd really rather that someone wasn't me. But I reckon it would be, given I'm well and truly outnumbered by the Bassett outfit.'

'It's so unfair that Jason Bassett and his son can get away with terrorizing everyone in Paradise.' She dabbed a handkerchief around her eyes to soak up the tears. 'You haven't even heard me sing yet, and I was so looking forward to singing for you.'

He had to admit that he had been looking forward to that too, and to leave without hearing her sing was something he would always regret. But in the end it was the only sensible thing to do.

He looked at the grandfather clock in the corner of the room. The morning was fast disappearing. 'I guess I'd best be heading off. It's been a pleasure to have met you, Laney Landers, and I'll always be in your debt for what you did for me.' He turned to go, but she grabbed him by the arm.

'I deserve a better farewell than that, Jed Grayson,' she said firmly, and then pulling his head down to hers, she kissed him tenderly on the lips.

CHAPTER SEVEN

Jed had left Paradise behind more than four hours earlier when he heard the commotion that was to change his plans forever. He had just rounded a prominent outcrop of rock and was about to ride down a draw into a small canyon when he heard a pair of rifles start firing in unison. Reining up he dismounted, and pulling his Winchester free of its scabbard, climbed atop the outcrop before peering anxiously down into the canyon below. Two riders sat astride their horses, one a big sorrel, the other a chestnut, and both men were pumping rounds through their Winchesters just as fast as the mechanics of their rifles would allow, the target for their lead being sixty head or so of prime beef.

Jed Grayson didn't hesitate. In fact he didn't even wait long enough to think it through. He knew well enough that what was going on down there wasn't right, so levering through a round he fired first one, then two, and finally three warning shots into the air to let those men know that what they were doing had been observed.

Two heads turned abruptly to look up at the outcrop, and no sooner had they spied Jed standing tall and imposing up there above them than they put spurs to their mounts, galloping off across the canyon to escape the threat of being shot.

Jed sat down on the rock and thought about what had just happened. If they were rustlers, why on earth would they be killing the cattle instead of selling them on for healthy profit? It just didn't make sense.

'Just keep still and don't make a grab for your weapon or I'll pull my trigger and worry about who you are later,' a male voice behind him demanded.

Jed froze. Sitting down as he was, he was completely at the mercy of whoever had crept up behind him.

'Stand up real slow and turn yourself around, I need to get a look at you.'

Jed did as he was told, and was stunned to find himself looking into the face of Thomas Thornton's foreman Jack Wilson, the man who had tried to hire him to work for his boss at the Circle D Ranch a few weeks back. By the look on Wilson's face he was just as surprised to see Jed.

'You're on Thornton land,' Wilson said. 'Maybe you'd like to explain to me why that is?'

'I didn't know I was,' Jed said truthfully. 'I'm heading for Wyoming and wasn't sure whose land I was travelling through.'

'It's customary to ask permission before you set foot on a man's land.'

'Like I said, I didn't know whose land I was on, so I couldn't ask.'

62

'What was the shooting I just heard?' Wilson demanded, his Henry rifle still pointing directly at Jed.

Jed inclined his head in the direction of the canyon. 'A couple of fellers were down there shooting into a bunch of beeves. I fired three shots in the air to scare them off.'

With the rifle trained on Jed, Wilson walked over to the rock, and stepping on to its flat top, peered down into the canyon. 'Dang it,' he said angrily when he spotted the dozen or so dead animals littering the canyon floor, 'that's Circle D beef.' He looked up in time to see two horsemen climbing their way over the top of the far end of the canyon. They were too far away for a bullet to reach them from this distance so he gave them up as a lost cause.

Jed cast a glance in the same direction. 'Any idea who they are?'

'They'll be Jason Bassett's men for sure,' Wilson said with disgust. 'I didn't think that even he would stoop so low as to resort to this.'

'Still trying to drive your boss off his ranch is he?'

'You guessed it. Obviously he's decided to step things up a mite.'

'I had a run-in with him myself this morning, that's why I'm heading for Wyoming.'

Wilson lowered his rifle. 'Sorry about the unfriendly welcome, but we've had a lot of trouble around here of late. I thought you might be working for Bassett.'

'He thought I was working for Thornton.'

'So you've been caught between a rock and a hard place.'

'You might say that.'

Jack Wilson looked into the canyon again. 'I'd say you've saved at least fifty head of Thornton cattle, warning those *hombres* off. Mr Thornton will be mighty appreciative of that. How about coming back to the ranch for a hot meal? It'll be dark in a few hours, so there's a bed in the bunkhouse for the night if you want it.'

A hot meal and a comfortable bed sounded much better than cold beans and a bedroll to Jed, and he concurred: 'I'll take you up on that offer.'

Wilson looked pleased. 'Good. Grab that gelding of yours and we'll head for the homestead. It's a good hour's ride from here, so the sooner we get going, the better.'

As Jed rode in through the main entrance to the Circle D Ranch he silently congratulated himself on agreeing to stay the night. Thick black rainclouds had gathered overhead and looked set to dump their heavy payload on any traveller who was unfortunate enough to be caught outside when the storm struck. He would be doubly pleased as he lay in his bed that night and listened to the rain hammering down on the bunkhouse roof.

'Come on up to the big house and meet Mr Thornton,' Jack said. 'He'll want to thank you for chasing Bassett's men off.'

Jed brushed down his dusty clothes as Jack opened the front door to the Thornton's big ranch house. He was no pleaser of men, but he didn't want to come across as just another saddle tramp when he met the owner of the second biggest ranch in the county.

A pretty girl descended the stairs towards them as Jack ushered Jed into the foyer. 'Hello, Jack,' she said sweetly, 'who is your friend?'

'Miss Rebecca Thornton, I'd like you to meet Mr Jed Grayson,' Jack said with formality.

Jed removed his Stetson and silently cursed himself for not having done so sooner. He would have had time to smooth his hair down properly if he had. It would no doubt be plastered down on his head due to the heat he had just ridden through. He might be no pleaser of men, but he certainly liked to make a good impression on the ladies, especially the pretty ones, and this one was mighty pretty indeed.

She smiled at him then, and it lit up her beautiful face to such an extent that he didn't doubt she had every man for miles around eating out of the palm of her hand.

'It's a pleasure to meet you, Mr Grayson.'

Jed gave a slight nod of his head, and said, 'And you too, Miss Thornton.'

'Jed's the feller who gave Zach Bassett the hiding of his life yesterday,' Jack said with a chuckle.

'Then I am more than pleased to meet you, Mr Grayson,' she said, the smile that hadn't left her lighting her face up even more.

Jack looked over her shoulder at an open door behind her. 'Is your pa home?'

'Yes, he's in there,' she said, noticing his eyes were trained on the door to her father's study.

'I'll take Jed in to meet him. Jed's just done the

Circle D a big favour that I think Mr Thornton should know about.'

Rebecca walked over to the doorway and poked her head inside. 'Jack's here with a gentleman he would like you to meet, Pa.'

'Send the pair of them in, sweetheart,' a pleasant-sounding voice answered.

As Rebecca stood to one side to let the two men through Jed couldn't help but notice the close scrutiny she subjected his face to as he passed by.

Thomas Thornton stood up and skirted round his desk to greet the stranger. 'I'm Thomas Thornton,' he said, extending his hand to Jed.

Jed grasped the big hand firmly. 'Jed Grayson.'

'Ah, the man who refused my offer of a job,' he said jovially.

'It seemed like the right thing to do at the time.'

'And now?'

'I'm heading for Wyoming,' he put in quickly, not liking where this was going. 'My uncle has a job waiting on his ranch for me.'

'I came across Jed above Willow Creek Canyon,' Jack explained. 'He'd just run off a couple of Bassett's men who were shooting Circle D beef.'

'Get many head?' Thornton asked with concern.

'About a dozen. It would have been upwards of sixty head if Jed hadn't intervened.'

'Then I'm much obliged to you, Mr Grayson,' Thornton said sincerely. 'We can ill afford to lose that many cattle at the moment.'

'I should think a rancher can ill afford to lose cattle

at any time, beef being his only means of making a living.'

'You're right about that. Unfortunately Jason Bassett has been putting the squeeze on us one way or another this past year or so, and now every single head of beef counts.'

'He's an arrogant self-serving cuss, that's for sure,' Jed said.

Thornton looked surprised. 'You've met him?'

'This morning. He came around to the boarding house I was staying at to teach me a lesson for whipping his boy.'

'And did he?'

Jed shook his head. 'I got the drop on him and sent him packing with his tail tucked firmly between his legs.'

'Good for you,' Thomas Thornton boomed.

'However, I did take it from my conversation with him that it might be a good idea to leave Paradise before I became a permanent resident.'

Thornton took his meaning. 'He would try to kill you if you'd stayed, that's for certain. Jason Thornton allows no man to better him and live long enough to pass on the tale to the next generation.'

'I figured that.'

'I offered Jed a meal and a bed down at the bunkhouse, Mr Thornton.'

'I think we can do better than that, Jack.' He walked over to the door and called for his daughter.

Rebecca Thornton swept into the room giving Jed his second look at her, and she was even more beautiful than he had thought she was the first time round.

'Yes, Pa?'

'Mr Grayson is going to be dining with us tonight, sweetheart, and can you get the guest room ready for him? He'll be spending the night as well.'

'The bunkhouse is good enough for me,' Jed put in quickly.

'Nonsense! We owe you a debt of gratitude for what you've done for us. Putting you up for the night is the very least we can do.'

Jed let it go. He would rather be down in the bunkhouse mixing with Thornton's ranch hands where he didn't have to be constantly watching his manners, but it wasn't worth offending the man or his daughter.

'I suspect you'd like to freshen up a little, seeing as you've been in the saddle all day.' He rang a little bell he had on his desk, and waited patiently for a minute or so until a robust woman with rolled-up sleeves and wearing a white apron entered the room.

'You rang for me, Mr Thornton?'

'Martha, Mr Grayson here is staying with us for the night. I'd like you to draw him a bath up in the guest room so he can bath before dinner is served.'

She glanced across at the big clock in the corner and realized if she was going to get that done before dinner she would have to hurry. 'I'll do that straightaway, Mr Thornton.'

'Best housekeeper we've ever had. We get her to do everything around the place that needs doing except for the cooking,' Thornton said after the woman had scurried off to accomplish the task. 'Come and sit down and I'll pour us some drinks while she's getting your bath ready.'

Jed felt rather underdressed later on at the dinner table. The Thorntons obviously favoured dressing up for the occasion, judging by the fancy duds they were wearing. Even Jack was wearing a suit and a string tie to go with it. But all Jed had was a clean set of clothes that were rather creased from being stuffed into his carpet bag.

'Rebecca has done most of the cooking since her ma passed away,' Thornton said during the meal when he saw Jed savouring a particularly tasty helping of blueberry and apple pie. 'I think you'll agree she's a dab hand at it.'

Jed swallowed the piece he had been eating and said, 'I think saying she's a dab hand would be an insult to her talents, Mr Thornton. She's second to none, in my opinion.'

Thomas Thornton looked pleased, and Jed suspected he was the sort of man who was very proud of the things in his life that meant something to him, his daughter obviously being at the top of that category.

'So how did all this business with Jason Bassett get started?' Jed asked, sure that he had now earned the older man's confidence.

Thomas Thornton sighed. 'Jason and I grew up together. We were actually friends during our childhood days. Right up into our early twenties, in fact.'

'And then something happened to change all that.'

'Jennifer Prescott happened.' He saw the puzzled look on Jed's face and smiled. 'Jennifer was Rebecca's ma.'

'And Bassett wanted her for himself?'

'You guessed it. She was the prettiest girl either of us had ever laid our eyes on.' He glanced across the table at his daughter. 'The likeness between Jennifer and Rebecca is uncanny.'

In that case Jed had no problem believing Jennifer had been the prettiest girl they had ever seen.

'At first she showed a preference for him, but when that temper of his started to show its ugly side she switched her affections to me, and it all ran from there. Jason was furious that I had the prettiest girl around on my arm, and threatened to cut all ties with me unless I relinquished my claim to her.'

'Which you didn't, I take it?'

Thornton chuckled. 'I was too much in love with her by that stage to ever do that. He shunned me after I refused. He wouldn't so much as lift his eyes up to look at me when we passed in the street. It was sad really. Twenty-three years of friendship just tossed aside like an oily rag.'

'And from there it escalated to what it is today?'

'It got worse after Jennifer died seven years ago. I think he blamed me for her death. She got caught in a rainstorm while coming back from Paradise and developed pneumonia. She died a week later. He turned up at the funeral and told me she would still be alive if she had married him, and maybe she would be. But that was the turning point when he started to play rough.'

'How exactly?'

'Cutting fences, damming up the creek to stop the water flowing to the two-hundred acre meadow, and just generally doing what he could to disrupt the successful running of the Circle D. It seems he's resorting to killing my livestock now.'

'He aims to get his hands on this ranch,' Jack cut in. 'That's his number one aim.'

'Now, Jack, we don't know that for sure,' Thornton said quickly.

'With all due respect, Mr Thornton, I believe we do. He's forced most of the smaller ranchers off their spreads, and now we're right on the boundary with his ranch. His hands talk pretty loosely when they're in town, too. They say he wants the Circle D real bad.'

'Liquored up cowboys'll say almost anything, Jack, you know that. I'm sure all it's about is getting back at me for marrying Jennifer.'

Jack shot Jed a glance that said . . . 'you can believe what I'm saying is the truth,' but didn't say so in front of his boss.

'Anyway,' Thornton continued, 'he's been a pain in my side for years now, especially with him constantly cutting the wires between our two ranches so his cattle can graze out our stored up grass. We need that grass to get us through the winter. That's why I sent Jack into town to try and hire you. We need a man who's good with his gun to frighten Jason's men into staying away from that fence. It's costing me a fortune to be continually repairing it.' He fixed his light brown eyes on Jed with renewed hope. 'You wouldn't consider taking that job on now you know why I want you, would you?'

'I'm sorry, Mr Thornton, but I don't want to get any more involved in this whole business than I already have. Besides, I promised my uncle I'd help him with his ranch, and I'm already a couple of weeks late in turning up.'

'I understand,' Thomas Thornton said with obvious disappointment. 'But I had to at least try.'

'There's never any harm in trying,' Jed conceded.

When Jed turned in for the night he did so with the knowledge that the next day he would be leaving the feud between the Thorntons and the Bassetts behind, and a brand new chapter in his life would be about to begin. He felt pleased about that, very pleased indeed.

CHAPTER EIGHT

'This horse ain't going anywhere with this hoof,' Jack Wilson said as he dropped the hind leg of Jed's gelding. 'He's gunna need three or four days of complete rest before it comes right.'

'Dang it,' Jed said with impatience in his voice. 'I'm already plenty late getting to Wyoming as it is. Uncle Tom isn't gunna be too impressed with me.'

'Not much that can be done about it, I'm afraid. You'll have to stay here and accept Mr Thornton's hospitality.'

'Don't get me wrong,' Jed said quickly. 'I'm grateful to Mr Thornton for putting me up. It's just that the harder I try to get to Wyoming, the more difficult it seems it becomes to actually get there.'

'Maybe somebody up there is trying to tell you something,' Jack said, as he straightened up, a wry smile on his lips.

Jed grinned at the comment. 'Now don't you try and bring the Almighty into this, Jack Wilson. I've got enough fellers wanting me to do their bidding without the good Lord getting involved too.'

'You can't blame a man for trying. Anyway, you're gunna be laid up at the Circle D for the next few days whether you like it or not, so you might as well get used to the idea.'

'I don't want to impose on the Thorntons' hospitality any more than I already have,' Jed confessed. 'How about I do a bit of work around here to earn my keep?'

Jack Wilson rubbed the stubble on his jaw as he thought the suggestion over. 'We could always do with an extra man helping out,' he conceded. 'We've been planning to send a man out to restock the line shacks with provisions but haven't been able to spare anyone yet.'

'I'm the man for the job, then,' Jed said firmly. 'Just point me in the right direction and I'll get right on to it.'

'I'll get one of the boys to organize a saddle horse and a couple of pack mules for you. There's six line shacks out there so it'll take you about three days to restock them and get yourself back here. We'll have your gelding fitter than a fiddle by the time you get back.'

'That's good enough for me,' Jed said brightly.

Jed lit out for the first line shack with nothing more than a crudely drafted map and a vague set of directions, but he was confident enough he would find the place before the sun had passed directly overhead. There was a beautiful clear sky that enhanced the beauty of the wide open range of the Circle D Ranch, and Jed was determined to enjoy his time out in the open. With his stock of tobacco replenished, and plenty of food packed on to the mules he had in tow, he certainly wouldn't be in need of anything.

He let his mind wander as he ambled along, and it wasn't long before it brought up the image of Miss Laney Landers. That beautiful face would be etched on his memory for the rest of his life now. Dang, but he felt bad about how she had fallen for him. He had even considered asking her to come with him to Wyoming, but there was no way a woman who had lived her entire life in town would consent to becoming a ranch hand's wife, even if it was his uncle who owned the ranch he worked on. It was too bad really, as Jed was sure she would have been a wife to be proud of. But then, those were the breaks, and a man had no choice but to accept his lot in life and do the best he could with it.

He doubted Laney would have been able to adjust to the drudgery of ranch life even if she had consented. She was a town woman, who had lived off the excitement of doing live shows for the patrons of the Silver Dollar Saloon. She would have missed the adulation and applause that she had become accustomed to. He didn't think he could have handled the pain of another woman leaving him, and he was sure that is what she would have done, once the reality of being his wife had kicked in. He would miss her though, what man wouldn't. She was everything a woman should be, and then more. But it was for the best. They would both be better off in the long run.

Jed reached the first line shack just before midday. The rusty old hinges of its warped door protested loudly as he put his shoulder to the timber and shoved it open. The mustiness of the shack's interior immediately assaulted his nostrils, and the copious quantities of rat droppings that covered not only the table and bunks, but the floor as well, added to the general unhealthiness of the place. Rummaging through the cupboards he discovered that even the labels on the tinned goods had been eaten by the rats, so it didn't take him long to realize he was going to have to do a whole heap more than just restock the place with food to get it ready for human habitation. It would be tomorrow morning at the earliest before he would be ready to head on to the second line shack.

He managed to get the fire going and so saved himself the indignity of having to eat cold beans for supper. Tomorrow he would see if he could shoot some game and have a meal of meat at the next line shack. He slept fitfully that night, courtesy of the hard bunk bed that was in sharp contrast to the soft warm bed he had been treated to back at the Thornton homestead.

He was up and gone early the next morning, determined to restock at least two more of the line shacks before darkness fell. He was an hour and a half's ride away from the shack he had just spent the night in when he came across a pack of wolves tearing at a carcase that lay on the ground beside a small brook that wound its way down the rocky slope he was traversing.

'Strange that one of Thornton's steers would be up here on its own,' he said to himself. He decided to ride on over and take a closer look.

The wolves slunk thirty yards or so away and snarled

their disapproval at being chased away from their meal as he dismounted and inspected the unfortunate beast. It was one of Thornton's cattle all right – the Circle D brand showed up clearly on its rump. It must have been left behind after the last muster, living wild and free on its lonesome, Jed figured. He was about to climb back into the saddle and continue on his way when something caught his attention and caused him to take an even closer look. Squatting down he gave his full attention to the beast's face.

There was no mistaking the small round hole punched through the steer's forehead. This animal had been shot, but its meat left here either to rot or be eaten by wolves and coyotes. That wouldn't be the work of one of Thornton's hands, so it must have been Bassett's men who had come all the way up here – but why? They must have known all they would find would be one or two strays and nothing more. If they wanted to give Thornton trouble, surely they would concentrate their efforts on his main herd down in the lowlands.

Jed cast his eyes around the spot to see if he could garner any clues. The remains of a fire lay fifteen yards or so to the right of the carcase, and after inspecting it Jed concluded it was no more than two days ago that it had been in use. He wandered back to the steer, and bending over, subjected it to a closer scrutiny than the first time.

A slight rope burn was visible around its neck, and it had a broken front leg that he hadn't noticed until now due to that particular leg being tucked mostly under the downed beast. What had happened was beginning to become clear, and straightening up, he began a more extensive examination of the ground all around the dead steer. Although it wasn't the best of surfaces for picking prints, he did see the occasional heel mark from a man's boot, and quite a few hoofprints, indicating there had been several cattle milling around this spot only a few days ago. It could mean only one thing: rustlers had been at work.

The dead steer had been roped, but had obviously busted its leg in the struggle and had been shot because of it. The fire over yonder had held the running irons used to change the Circle D brand to the Bassett brand. It must mean Bassett's men had cut Thornton cattle out of the main herd down in the lowlands, and had driven them up here to change their brand. What they did with them next was anybody's guess – either they mixed them in with the Bassett herd, or they took them over the state line and sold them. Whatever the outcome, it still spelled financial loss for the Circle D Ranch and the Thornton family.

Placing his left hand on the saddle horn of his mare, Jed slipped his foot into the stirrup and pulled his weight up on to her back. It would be a couple of days before he had restocked the line shacks and got back to the ranch to alert Thomas Thornton to what was going on up here, but the sooner he got on with the job, then the sooner he would get back to divulge what he had just discovered.

He ran across the second line shack two hours later, and since it was in much better shape than the first he took no more than an hour to clean it out and restock it, then headed directly for the third, hoping to reach it by early afternoon. He had just navigated his way around a narrow rocky trail that snaked across the mountain and emerged on to a table top boasting ten acres or so of fertile mountainside, when he ran smack bang into a fellow butchering a small steer he had strung up from a branch of a sturdy tree. Jed didn't know who was surprised the most, him or the other fellow, but it was the other chap who went for his gun first, and so without hesitating Jed reached for his Navy Colt, and flipping it free and cocking back the hammer left the man in no doubt that if he finished his draw then he would soon be a dead man.

'Who are you?' the startled man asked with a shaky voice.

'I think that's the question I should be asking you, mister. You're on Thornton land, and if I'm not much mistaken that's Thornton beef you're cutting into.'

The fellow let his pistol slip back into its holster.

'I'm waiting,' Jed said tersely.

'Drop that six-gun!'

Jed swivelled in the saddle and fired without even bothering to identify his target. If they were Bassett's men then they wouldn't leave him alive to tell tales. His bullet hit home despite the fact he hadn't had time to take aim, and as Bassett's man sank to his knees Jed rounded on the first man who had reached for his gun again.

Hot lead struck Jed's saddle horn, ripping it clear of the saddle and sending it spiralling away, but not before a burning sensation sliced its way across Jed's left hip. The hasty shot gave Jed the time he needed to take his time and make his shot count. When his six-gun barked again another of Bassett's men lay face down on the ground.

Jed's free hand probed the wounded hip. It hurt like blazes but fortunately it hadn't done much more than graze him. The saddle horn must have taken most of the kick out of the bullet, and the angle it was fired from meant it had travelled across his body instead of entering his gut. He was about as lucky as a man could get. Untying his neckerchief he stuffed it down his waistband to sit over the wound, in the hopes it would staunch the flow of blood, before getting down from his horse and making sure Bassett's two men were dead.

Walking out on to the table top his suspicions were realized as he wandered amongst the eighty or so head busily employed in cropping the lush, knee-high grass. There was at least three days feed for this number of cattle, and Jed figured they were being held here until more of Bassett's men arrived to help drive them off the mountain and on to somewhere they could be sold.

He would have to abandon the restocking of the rest of the line shacks. It was more important to get word to Thornton that eighty of his head were up here so he could send men up to fetch them before Bassett's men arrived and beat them to it. Eighty head would be a sizeable number to lose, and the Circle D Ranch could ill afford the financial loss that that would entail. Stripping the provisions off the two mules he left them to graze amongst the herd, then climbed back into the saddle and made for the narrow pass that would take him off the table top and back down the mountain to the Thornton homestead.

CHAPTER NINE

'So Bassett's been rustling our beef as well as shooting them,' Thomas Thornton said as he handed Jed a glass containing a generous amount of whiskey. 'I guess he steals the ones he can get safely off our range without being seen and shoots those he can't. The end result is the same. He bankrupts us, destroying what I've taken years to build up, getting his revenge on me, then getting his hands on the Circle D when I'm forced to sell up.'

Jed nodded before taking a sip of his whiskey. If there was one thing Thomas Thornton was good at, it was stocking the finest of whiskey, and this time was no exception.

'And you said you shot some of his men?'

Jed sat the glass down on the table beside the armchair he was comfortably seated in. 'Two of them,' he divulged. 'I didn't have time to bury them, so they're lying exposed up there on the mountain I'm afraid. I hope the wolves don't get them before we can get back and sort them out.'

'Don't you go feeling bad about that,' Thornton said adamantly. 'They knew the risks they were taking when they stole those cattle – every cattle thief in this county knows what can happen to him if he goes down that particular trail.'

'So are we gunna head on up there to bring those cattle back down nearer the homestead?'

'At first light tomorrow I'll send some of the boys up there. But I think I'd like to keep you down here with me while they're doing that. I wouldn't put it past Bassett to attack the homestead if he knows I'm short-handed.'

That made sense. Bassett would have a man watching every movement to and from the Thornton homestead. He might just be crazy enough to attempt something like that if he knew Thornton was there with only a handful of men.

'Jack can see those cattle get back down here safely. He's a good man, is Jack Wilson, the best ramrod I've ever had on the Circle D. I can leave everything to him with total confidence that he'll come up trumps every time.'

'You're lucky to have him, then.'

'Don't I know it. I pay him accordingly, too. I've never paid a man as much as I pay Jack.'

Jed offered no objection as Thornton reached over with the bottle and topped up his glass.

'The main reason I want you close to the house is to keep an eye on Rebecca. She's a headstrong gal, is that one, the spitting image of her mother in both looks and temperament. The trouble is, I can't seem to stop her

83

from going riding out on the ranch on her own, and that worries me, with Bassett's men coming on to the Circle D uninvited. If one or more of them came across her there's no telling what they might do to her.'

Jed had a pretty fair idea what would happen to her, but he thought it best to say nothing to Thornton. 'I can hang around for another three or four days I suppose,' he said before knocking back another shot of whiskey.

'I'd be much obliged if you would. Now that we know what it is Bassett's men have been up to, everything must come to a head one way or another before the week is out. I don't want to get you killed or anything, but I figure you're mighty handy with a gun, and that might just swing things in our favour if it came down to lead being exchanged.'

'I didn't want to get myself involved in this,' Jed admitted. 'But what with the business that's gone on between Zach Bassett and me, and the fact I've just killed two of Jason Bassett's men, I figure I'm in this up to my neck. So you can count on me if the shooting starts before I head off to Wyoming.'

Thomas Thornton's face broke out into the broadest of smiles. 'I knew you were a man of integrity the very first time I laid eyes on you. Some men just have honesty and integrity written all over their faces, and you happen to be one of them, Jed Grayson.'

Jed downed the last of the whiskey in his glass and tried hard not to glance at the bottle still nestled in his host's hand. He didn't want to come across like he was trying to squeeze another drink out of the situation, even though he hoped Thornton would upend that bottle and tip what was left of its contents into Jed's glass without any prompting. 'I appreciate the compliment, Mr Thornton.'

'It's time you called me Tom,' Thornton said, and then did exactly what Jed had hoped he would, and drained all but the last few drops of whiskey from that bottle into Jed's glass. 'When I take to a man like I've taken to you then I insist everything is on a first name basis only.'

'If that's your rule, then who am I to object?' Jed said, before happily tipping more of that delicious whiskey down his throat.

Jed spotted the white mare streaking off across the meadow below the ranch house several seconds before he realized who the rider was. In her buckskin riding outfit, and with her long black hair streaming out behind her, Rebecca Thornton looked surprisingly like a carefree Indian maiden racing her pony across her tribe's hunting grounds.

Jed sighed as he dropped the rag he was using to oil his saddle and headed to the corral to catch a horse. If Thomas Thornton wanted him to keep a close eye on his daughter then he would have to follow her at a discreet distance to make sure she didn't run into any trouble. He just hoped she didn't intend to stay out there for too long, as he had other things he would rather be doing than minding the girl.

Jed caught a frisky-looking sorrel that looked like it could run. The gelding wasn't overly big but he was sleek and designed for speed. Rebecca shouldn't be able to get away from him if he was seated on that particular beast. Saddling up just as fast as he could without upsetting his mount, Jed was soon on the sorrel's back and heading out of the yard and towards the meadow where he had last seen Rebecca.

Ten minutes had elapsed before the girl came into sight again. She had left the meadow behind and was carefully picking her way down a draw that led to a shallow, rocky-bottomed river. With the day being a particularly hot one Jed just hoped she wasn't intending on stripping off and going for a swim. If she caught him spying on her there would be hell to pay, and he didn't think even Thomas Thornton would look favourably upon it, despite the fact it had been his idea that Jed should keep the girl within sight at all times.

Jed reined in his gelding and watched Rebecca's progress from the cover of a grove of cottonwoods. Her shapely figure bobbed ever so slightly up and down with every step her mare took, and even from this distance she was a vision of femininity that could hold a man firmly in her spell.

The white mare reached the water's edge, and with its rider loosening her grip on the reins the horse bent its head down to drink. A few seconds later Rebecca slipped lithely from the animals back and without so much as glancing around began to strip off her buckskin garments.

'Dang it!' Jed said aloud, as his fears were being realized. He knew he should look away, but the lure of a beautiful young woman soon being completely naked not more than a stone's throw away drove all thoughts of propriety from his mind.

Rebecca's pale skin shone white and alluring in the bright sunshine as she twisted up her long hair then tied it securely. Jed's heart beat rapidly as the blood began to rise in his veins. She was about as beautiful as a woman could get, her body perfectly proportioned, and in its first flush of full womanhood. With a sudden rush of guilt Jed Grayson tore his eyes away from the charming vision. He was better than that. Or at least he felt he should be. Maybe he wasn't quite the decent fellow he had always prided himself on being after all. Dismounting, he sat in the shade with his back against a tree where he could no longer see her and patiently waited for her to enjoy her swim. As soon as he heard the splashing of the water stop he would give her a few minutes to get dressed before casting his eyes in her direction again.

Jed opened his eyes with a start. Dang it, he had fallen asleep, and judging by the angle of the sun he had been slumbering for nearly an hour. Leaping to his feet he discovered to his alarm that the white mare was gone, and along with it the young woman he had promised he would not lose track of. Leaping up on to the back of the gelding, Jed Grayson urged him forwards, hoping against hope that the girl wasn't so far ahead that he wouldn't be able to pick up her trail. He would never be able to face Thomas Thornton again if anything happened to his precious daughter.

Down at the river's edge Jed searched frantically for

where the girl had crossed over, finally finding the spot several hundred yards downstream where the river widened but became considerably shallower. He hurried the gelding over. Time was of the utmost importance now. The girl had such a head start on him that the only way he would catch up to her would be to push his mount hard despite running the risk of bringing him up lame.

The white mare's prints could be seen where she had climbed out of the river and scrambled up a dirt bank to enter a small wood higher up, the rustling of the leaves in the gentle breeze reaching Jed's ears even before his gelding had tackled the steep bank.

Rebecca would still be blissfully unaware that anyone was following her, Jed mused, and that was probably for the best. If she really was the headstrong type like her father claimed, the knowledge that Jed was on her tail might be enough to prompt her to cover her tracks, and then he wouldn't have a snowball's chance in hell of catching up to her. As it was, it was going to be tough enough to close the gap, despite her ignorance of the fact he was after her.

Jed had left the wood behind, crossed a small plain and entered a pass at the base of a mountain range before he noticed the tracks from Rebecca's mare were looking fresher. Breathing a sigh of relief Jed calculated he might be in sight of her sometime in the next fifteen minutes. Maybe everything was going to end on a good note after all.

Jed's first inkling that all was not well was when he saw two sets of hoofprints. Either Rebecca had ridden all the way out here to meet up with a lover, or someone had happened upon her and was now accompanying her. The first scenario Jed thought was highly unlikely, so that only left the second possibility. Whether that someone was friend or foe Jed was yet to discover, but at least now that he was not far behind he could offer her help if it proved she were in need of it.

A dry lump formed in Jed's throat when he came across the white mare abandoned, and not because she was suffering from the effects of lameness either, for she was perfectly sound in limb and nibbling at what little rough grass she could find poking up through the rocky ground of the pass. Jed could see marks in the dust that looked suspiciously like someone had been dragged over to where another horse had been standing. That meant Rebecca was in trouble. Someone had taken her. Someone she did not want to be with, and so Jed must find her soon, before the unthinkable happened to her.

Deep in the pass he came across a big chestnut stallion, its reins dragging on the ground as if its rider had abandoned it in a hurry. Glancing all around Jed desperately tried to figure out what was going on. Whoever had Rebecca must have continued on foot – but why, when they had a perfectly sound horse right here?

A scream pierced the silence of the isolated pass and reverberated around its solid walls, sending a cold shiver racing up Jed Grayson's spine. That answered the question as to the abandoned horse, and there were no prizes for guessing what Rebecca's captor was attempting to do – but would Jed be able to locate the girl in time to save her?

Leaving his mount behind, Jed headed towards where the scream had originated, and was rewarded by yet another, which confirmed he was on the right track. Slipping through a narrow gap between two towering chunks of rock, he emerged into a small amphitheatre completely shielded from the outside world by the rock walls that enclosed it. With her back against a large boulder, not more than twenty yards away, was Rebecca, and she was frantically struggling with a big man who was doing everything in his power to strip her of her clothing.

Jed's Navy Colt sprang into his hand. 'Leave her be!' he bellowed, his stern voice echoing eerily around the small arena.

The man pushed himself away from Rebecca and spun round to counter the unexpected threat with surprise written all over his face. He had obviously expected to have his way with the pretty girl without any interference from anyone. 'Who are you?' he growled menacingly, even though he hadn't missed seeing the pistol pointed directly at him.

'Move out of the way quickly, Rebecca!' Jed bellowed.

Despite the ordeal she had just been through Rebecca had enough presence of mind to obey immediately, and although the man made a sudden grab for her in the hopes of using her for a shield against the danger that had just presented itself, he was too slow, the girl skipping well out of his reach, leaving Jed holding the upper hand.

'I don't have any time for a brute who forces himself

90

on to a woman,' Jed said with venom, his pulse rate soaring as he listened to the girl sobbing uncontrollably somewhere off to his left.

Six foot one or thereabouts, with a swarthy complexion and a long drooping moustache and unkempt black hair, the fellow glared back at Jed as if he had no right to interfere in what he figured had been his good fortune. 'What do you care?' he snarled. 'You're bound to take your turn at her, ain't you?'

Jed's trembling hand thumbed back the hammer on the Colt. 'Talk like that is not doing your chances of walking away from this any good at all.'

The man's hand was hovering very close to the butt of his six-gun, and feeling about him the way he did Jed hoped he would be foolish enough to attempt to draw it. It would give him all the excuse he needed to bring the hammer down on his own pistol, and he sorely wanted to bring that hammer down on this piece of scum.

'Rebecca,' Jed said softly, 'I need you to go back out to where my horse is and wait for me there.'

Rebecca said nothing, she merely walked towards the gap Jed had just come through, sobbing as she went, and within seconds had disappeared from sight as well as sound.

'You're one of Bassett's men I take it?' Jed said curtly.

'What of it?'

'Does he know you're up here trying to have your way with innocent young girls out riding on their own land?'

'He hates the Thorntons. He don't care if I have a

little fun with Thornton's daughter.'

'But I do,' Jed said evenly. 'And now we're faced with a bit of a dilemma, aren't we?'

Bassett's man looked at him with incomprehension in his steely grey eyes.

'If I let you go, Rebecca's gunna be fearing you turning up again some time when she least expects it, to try and finish what you've started. And when you stop to think about it, there's really nothing to stop you from doing just that, is there? Except me, of course.'

The grey eyes narrowed somewhat. 'You telling me you're prepared to shoot me without giving me a chance to defend myself?'

'I'm giving you as much chance as you gave the girl. You were armed as well as being much bigger and stronger than her. That didn't stop you from going ahead with what you tried to do.'

'That's different.'

'Not in my book it ain't.'

'I wasn't gunna kill her, just have some fun with her.'

'Fun for you maybe. But it would have ruined her life. Now, I aim to give her life back to her.'

Realizing his fate was sealed, Bassett's man took the only option left open to him: snatching at his six-gun he tried to clear leather and squeeze off a shot before the hammer came down on Jed's Colt.

The pistol in Jed Grayson's hand roared out its answer to the challenge, and Bassett's man took the full force of its fury in the middle of his chest. Dropping his own weapon he staggered forwards a few faltering steps, a look of bewilderment on his face. It was as if he couldn't understand how it had come to this. One moment he was about to enjoy the delights that a young woman's body had to offer, and the next he was about to draw his final breath on this earth. With that same look still on his face he suddenly pitched forwards, and after a moment or two of involuntary twitching, lay perfectly still on the hard ground at Jed's feet.

CHAPTER TEN

As he emerged from the gap, a bullet glanced off the rock to the right of his head and whined off into the distance. 'Rebecca, it's me, Jed Grayson!' Jed hollered quickly, hoping the girl would realize her mistake and drop the rifle she was holding to allow him to advance safely.

Still sobbing, she slipped the Winchester back into the scabbard on Jed's saddle horse and waited for him to join her. 'I thought it was him,' she said tearfully.

'He's dead,' Jed said gently. 'He ain't ever gunna give you trouble again.'

Rushing towards him, she threw her arms around his neck and clung to him for all she was worth.

'You're safe now,' he said uncomfortably, not being accustomed to this sort of reaction from a woman.

'Thank you,' she said, nestling in even closer.

It had been years since a woman had snuggled herself this close against his body, especially one as well endowed as Rebecca, and it began to stir parts of him that hadn't been stirred in a very long time. Not giving her more than a few seconds to compose herself, he pulled away and made like he was preparing the horse for the ride back to the ranch house.

'Pa will want to reward you for this,' she said, her sobbing now under control.

'No reward necessary,' Jed said in a businesslike fashion, hoping to put an end to the emotional scene she was creating.

'He was going to . . . going to . . .'

'I know what he was going to do,' Jed said, turning around and looking into her face for the first time. 'Let's just forget about it, shall we? You're safe now and that's all that matters.'

'I can't forget about it. I'll never forget what you've done for me.'

'Let's get moving,' he said abruptly, and then clutching the reins of his horse, began to walk off down the trail towards where the white mare was grazing.

'You are a remarkable man,' Rebecca said, after she had mounted her mare and the pair had ridden quite some distance from the pass.

Jed said nothing, but just continued to stare straight ahead as if he were studying something important on the horizon.

'I take it my father sent you out here to keep watch over me.'

Jed pretended not to hear.

'You don't have to answer – I know he did. He's always been very protective of me, especially after Ma died.'

This time Jed turned in the saddle to look at her. 'It's

95

just as well for you he is.'

She smiled engagingly at him. 'I'm glad you've decided to speak to me at last. And yes, you are right, I am lucky he is protective of me. And he certainly picked the right man for the job of watching over me.' She hesitated for a moment. 'Were you watching me when I went for a swim in the river earlier on?'

Jed looked away, hoping she wouldn't see the guilt in his eyes.

'I don't mind if you were.'

He didn't know how to answer that one. She had seemed to be so prim and proper when he had first met her. The upbringing her father had chosen had fashioned a lady out of her, but here she was admitting to Jed she didn't mind if he had been spying on her frolicking naked.

'Do I shock you, Mr Grayson?' She sounded a little sad.

He shook his head. The truth was, he didn't know whether to be shocked or not.

'I knew you were different the moment I first saw you,' she went on. 'You are not like the men I am used to. I can sense you have been through things that have hurt you. Things that have changed you, too, I think.'

Jed's mind began to turn over what she was saying mighty fast. How could she possibly know that? Could she read his mind?

'You are more sensitive towards a woman. I knew that straightaway.'

She couldn't possibly. They had hardly spoken more than a dozen or so words to one another in the time he had been at the Circle D Ranch.

'You aren't the only one who's been watching someone,' she confessed. 'I've watched you closely, too, as you went about your chores. The window to my bedroom overlooks the barnyard.'

He squirmed a little in his saddle, the leather squeaking out in protest each time he shifted his weight.

'I hope you will decide to stay on at the Circle D, Jed,' it was the first time she had used his Christian name. 'Pa could use a man like you to help run the ranch.'

'He's got Jack Wilson for that,' Jed said unemotionally.

'And Jack is a good man too. But he lacks the sort of grit that you've got.'

'Jack Wilson is just as capable as I am.'

'You have trouble taking a compliment don't you?'

'Not if it's a deserved one.' Reining in his gelding he reached across and grabbed hold of the bridle on the white mare bringing her to a standstill beside him. 'I've just stopped something horrible from happening to you, and I understand that you're feeling like you're in my debt. But there really is no need to carry on like this.'

She looked a little crestfallen. 'You have mistaken my admiration for gratitude. I like you for who you are, Jed, not because you saved me, though I am grateful for that.' Without saying another word she dug her mare in the ribs and left him sitting astride the gelding staring after her, as she cantered across the prairie towards the Thornton homestead.

'I can't thank you enough,' Thomas Thornton said, as he held out the glass of whiskey to Jed that had become a nightly treat. 'Rebecca told me how terrified she was and how close she came to . . . well, you know what I mean without me having to say it.'

Jed nodded.

'I know you're determined to head on to Wyoming and throw in your lot with your uncle, but I'd like to ask you if you'd consider hanging around here for another couple of weeks. I'm sure Bassett's gunna try something to bring it all to a head, and without someone like you here I fear he'll succeed.' Thornton plonked himself down in the armchair beside Jed's. 'It's a lot I'm asking from you, I know that. But I've got no one else to turn to. And then there's Rebecca to consider.' He shot a sideways glance at Jed to gauge if his last remark had hit home or not.

Although Jed wanted nothing more than to start his new life in Wyoming as soon as possible, what Jason Bassett and his men had done sickened him to his very stomach, and now he didn't feel he could just walk away and leave the Thorntons to face what lay ahead on their own. 'I guess I can put off Uncle Tom for a while longer.'

'Splendid!' Thornton topped Jed's glass up again. It was an action Jed had come to expect now, and one he certainly had no objection to. 'Your gelding is no longer lame, by the way.'

'That's good. I have to admit I've felt a little lost without him.'

Rebecca walked into the room just then, and the smile she flashed at Jed said it all. She was a woman in love, and she didn't care if the whole world knew it, not even her father. 'Good evening, Jed,' she said warmly.

Jed nodded in her direction without allowing too much in the way of eye contact. 'Evening, Rebecca.'

'I was wondering if you would join me out on the front porch for half an hour or so. The stars are looking spectacular tonight.'

Jed shot a nervous look in Thomas Thornton's direction, but the older man just grinned.

'Don't let me stand in the way of you two youngsters enjoying the evening,' he said.

It was then that Jed realized Rebecca's father wasn't only aware of his daughter's feelings for his guest, but he actually approved of them, too.

With the greatest of reluctance Jed got up from his comfortable chair, and feeling obligated to leave his glass of whiskey behind, followed the young beauty out on to the front porch.

'Pa taught me the names of all the major stars when I was a girl,' Rebecca said when they had settled into the swing seat that took up pride of place on the porch. She began to name them aloud.

'I know the stars, Rebecca,' Jed said, cutting her off before she could finish. 'I've spent a lifetime out beneath them.'

She looked a little shocked at his abruptness.

'Where is all this heading?' he asked bluntly.

'Straight to the point,' she said and then smiled. 'I think that's one of the traits I like the most about you.'

99

'And the answer to my question is. . . ?'

'If I was to wait for you to make a move I would grow old waiting, so I've decided to broach the subject myself.'

Jed's stomach began to twist itself up in knots. This was something he hadn't been expecting. He knew the girl had a crush on him, but he had figured if he just kept out of her way until he left for Wyoming, then any problems would be averted. He hadn't counted on her taking the initiative.

'As you know, Pa doesn't have a son, and I'm his only daughter. As such, I stand to inherit the Circle D Ranch someday.'

Those knots in his stomach were tightening even further.

'Whoever I choose to marry gets a ranch into the bargain.' She paused for a moment to allow the full meaning of what she had just said to sink in. 'Of course, like any well bred girl I'd like to be courted first.' She turned her stunning eyes on him now, and he found it impossible not to stare into their depths. 'I would like the man who courts me to be you.'

It took a while for Jed's head to process the information. Was she saying she wanted to marry him and the ranch came with the deal?

'And what does your father have to say about all this?' he said eventually.

'I have discussed it with him, and he has given me his blessing.'

Jed leaned forwards in his seat and stared off into the dark night. 'How old are you, Rebecca?'

'Twenty-one.'

'How old do you think I am?'

'Twenty-nine . . . thirty maybe.'

'I'm thirty-two. Don't you think that's a little too old for you?'

She shook her lovely head. 'Age isn't important when two people are in love with each other.'

'But I'm not in love with you,' he said frankly.

'Not at the moment maybe. But I hope you will come to love me in time.'

'And the ranch is the carrot you dangle in front of me to get me interested?'

She looked hurt by his comment, and so he instantly regretted having said it.

'I was merely letting you know how things would be if you were to decide you liked me as much as I like you,' she said a little shakily, her former confidence beginning to desert her.

'I'm sorry, Rebecca, that was unkind of me.'

'I have had so many men come calling,' she confessed, 'but you are the only one who touches me here,' she placed her pale hand over her heart.

'I'm not a refined man, Rebecca. I don't carry any airs or graces about my person.'

'And I love that about you. You're refreshingly honest.'

'Eleven years is quite an age difference.'

'Pa was nine years older than Ma, and they were very happy together,' she pointed out.

He obviously wasn't going to get her to see sense by using that argument.

'We could build a wonderful life here together. I would give you sons to help you on the ranch, and maybe a daughter or two to look after you in your old age if you outlive me.'

'It sounds as if you've got it all worked out.'

'We would work it out together, Jed. I'm not the sort of woman who would try to control her husband. I would want you to take the lead. You are the type of man I would happily follow, if you would only give me the chance.'

The only way to handle this was to tell her he would think about it, and then maybe she would give him the space he needed to sort out this threat from the Bassetts before he left for Wyoming. She would cry for a while after he had gone, but she was young and would get over it soon enough. It wouldn't be long before another man came along who captured her fancy, and then she would forget that Jed Grayson had ever existed.

'Let me think about it for a week or so,' he said.

'That's all I ask.' She leaned across and kissed him on the mouth so quickly he didn't even see it coming. 'I'll leave you to your thoughts.' She got up from the swing and made her way to the door before looking back at him. 'I really would make you a good wife,' she said, then disappeared inside, leaving the tingle of her kiss still fresh on his lips.

CHAPTER ELEVEN

Jed had gone into town with a few of the Circle D hands to buy stores for the ranch. It was a case of safety in numbers. Having beaten the tar out of young Zach Bassett, Jed would be a target for any man who wanted to curry favour with the boy's father. He was coming out of Sorenson's Mercantile when he ran into Laney Landers.

'Hello, Laney,' he said, as she stood on the board-walk, the shock at seeing him standing as large as life right in front of her registering on her pretty face.

'Jed . . . I thought you had gone to Wyoming.'

'I did start out for Wyoming but I never actually got there,' he answered sheepishly.

'So where have you been these past two weeks?'

'At the Thorntons' ranch.'

'The Thorntons . . . what are you doing there?'

'It's a long story, Laney. But I'm gunna be staying out there for a few weeks more before I head off for my uncle's ranch.'

The shocked look was replaced by a hurt one. 'You've been out at the Thorntons for two whole weeks and you haven't once ridden into Paradise to see me?'

'I've had a lot to do, Laney,' he said uncomfortably.

'You could have spared an evening or two. It would have given you the opportunity to hear me sing.'

He didn't know what to say. She was right of course; she had been so good to him during the period of his convalescence that the very least he owed her was the effort to ride into town once or twice to spend an hour or two in her company.

'I thought I meant more to you than that.'

'You do, Laney. It's just there's so much going on at the moment with all this trouble coming from the Bassetts that I hardly have enough time for myself, let alone anyone else.'

He knew he had said the wrong thing when he saw the solitary tear slip from the corner of her eye and roll lazily down her cheek to balance precariously on the end of her chin.

'All right, Jed,' she said sadly, then pushing past him she scurried off down the boardwalk before he could see the tears come thick and fast.

'Dang it,' Jed muttered, being more than a little angry with himself that he had handled the situation so badly. The truth was, he liked the woman very much, and if things had been different then maybe he would have been in a position to do a whole lot more than just visit her once in a while. But things weren't different. Things were hanging in the balance, and he couldn't afford to have any distractions that might cost him his life. Laney Landers was a distraction. She mightn't realize the effect she had on men, but Jed knew. If

104

anyone knew how distracting she could be, it was Jed Grayson.

Laney had disappeared from sight before Jed spotted an unwelcome figure: Zach Bassett was standing in the darkened doorway of the gunsmith's shop, and had been watching the encounter between Jed and Laney with interest. His wounds now mostly healed from the beating he had taken three weeks back, he glared across the street at Jed with about as much hatred as a defeated man could muster. He was waiting for the opportunity to get his own back on his enemy, Jed had no doubts on that score.

Keeping one eye on Bassett, Jed walked off down the boardwalk to join the rest of the Circle D men outside the blacksmith's where they were getting some horses shod before returning to the ranch.

Two miles out of Paradise Jed reined up his gelding, lifted his canteen, then pulling the cork, took a swallow of the sun-warmed water.

'You all right, Jed?' Jack Wilson called over his shoulder as his horse slowly plodded on ahead.

'I'll catch up with you in a minute, Jack,' Jed answered. 'I'm just wetting my whistle.'

He had just replaced the canteen when he saw the briefest flash of sun on metal, and with an instinct honed by experience, immediately rolled out of the saddle. A bullet whistled over the spot where moments before he had been sitting astride his saddle horse, ending up somewhere amongst the trees away to his left. But it had been such a close thing that he doubted the shooter would have been aware that he had missed his target. As men and horses scattered in all directions Jed remained where he was, lying unmoving on the sun-baked ground, pretending for all he was worth that he was dead.

But the sound of hoofbeats betrayed the fact that whoever had fired that shot was leaving the scene of his crime with the greatest of haste, so leaping up from the ground, Jed mounted his gelding and gave chase.

A grey stallion streaked across the clearing in the trees up ahead – Jed figured he was heading for the rocky terrain a half mile distant where a man could conceal himself from an attack. Zach Bassett, if indeed it was him, had made a serious mistake when his bullet had missed Jed back there, because unless he made it to the safety of those rocks before Jed caught up with him, then he was going to pay for it with his life.

Jed leaned forwards across the lower half of his gelding's neck and urged him on. 'Come on, boy,' he coaxed, 'don't let him get away with it.'

The gelding responded by stretching out his long legs and giving it his all. If the stallion up ahead was going to have any chance of winning this race he was going to have to dig much deeper than he was already. And within minutes it was obvious to Jed that he was gaining on him. He was close enough to hear Bassett's horse straining to suck enough air into his big lungs to keep them operating, and although his own gelding was breathing hard, he wasn't struggling like the stallion was. It was only a matter of time now – Bassett wasn't going to beat him to those rocks after all.

The stallion stumbled, then regained his footing,

and stumbling again, conceded valuable ground to the rapidly pursuing gelding. Jed was only half a dozen lengths behind him now.

Bassett glanced over his shoulder to see his nemesis had closed the gap significantly, so brutally driving his spurs into the stallion's unprotected flanks he did his utmost to force a miracle out of the hapless beast.

A minute later Jed's gelding had drawn up alongside, causing the two horses' flanks to rub against one another as they hurtled recklessly forwards. Knowing it was now or never, Jed launched himself out of the saddle, and wrapping his strong arms around Zach Bassett's torso, wrenched him clear of his mount to land with a thump on the hard ground.

Jed was on his feet first, Bassett having taken the brunt of the fall as Jed had landed uppermost. But Zach knew that his life depended on him being able to face this new threat immediately, so ignoring the pain in his back he half scrambled, half threw himself at Jed's legs, knocking him down and pouncing on him with all the vigour of a cougar. Then over and over the two men rolled, each trying to pin the other's arms in a desperate attempt to gain ascendency.

Then Bassett let go with one hand, in order to make a grab for the knife in his boot. He fell just short of driving the blade into his foe's chest as Jed's hand closed around his wrist and forced the tip away.

Bassett uttered a sudden squeal of pain, forcing him to drop the knife as his wrist twisted abnormally, causing a burning sensation to run all the way to his elbow. He didn't have the luxury of checking to see if it was broken: he knew he must do all he could to end this contest now before Jed Grayson ended it for him.

Swinging his head forwards, he caught Jed flush in the face with his forehead, eliciting not only a grunt of pain from the older man, but a momentary lapse in concentration as well. Taking advantage of Jed's hands no longer gripping him tight he sprang to his feet and made a play for the Remington nestled in the holster on his hip.

Jed saw it coming and so rolled away a split second before the bullet kicked up the dust on the ground where he had just been lying. Sweeping his Navy Colt clear of its leather confines he returned fire from his prone position, hitting the youngster in the left shoulder.

'Don't!' he barked, as, stumbling backwards, Zach thumbed back the hammer for a second shot.

If Zach Bassett had heard the shouted command he certainly didn't show it, and as the Remington came up level Jed had no alternative but to fire again, this time the slug lodging itself deep in the boy's chest. With a cough that brought blood to his lips, Zachary Bassett looked down at Jed with fear in his eyes: he knew that what had just happened wasn't good, it wasn't good at all, so letting the pistol slip from his fingers he tried to stagger away from the conflict in a fruitless attempt to find somewhere safe to lick his wounds.

Jed was on his feet instantly. If Bassett was still standing, then he was still a threat. Not more than four minutes ago he had tried to ambush him, hadn't he? Striding over to the lurching man he clicked the hammer back on his Colt and aimed it at the back of Zach Bassett's head.

Turning his head just enough to see if he was being followed, Bassett saw the six-gun levelled at him and knew his flight was over. With a face expressing both pain and dejection he slowly shuffled around to accept his inevitable fate.

Jed Grayson's gun barrel was only inches from Bassett's forehead when the passion of battle left him and was supplanted by mercy. The boy looked so lost that despite the fact Bassett had just tried to kill him, Jed's heart went out to the lad. Slipping the gun back in his holster he was in time to catch the youngster as his legs gave way.

Lying him tenderly on the ground, he knelt down beside him as he struggled to draw in a breath. 'Is there anything you want me to tell your pa?' he asked gently.

Hatred filled the boy's eyes. 'Pa is gunna kill you for this,' he rasped out.

Jed sighed. Even in the throes of death the young fool couldn't find it in him to feel any sense of remorse. He watched the light of life go out in the boy's eyes, and realized that this conflict was about to go to a whole new level. The Bassett-Thornton feud would only end when one or both families were totally wiped out. Getting to his feet, Jed Grayson turned, and with a heavy heart, walked over to pick up the trailing reins of his gelding.

CHAPTER TWELVE

'Word in town is Jason Bassett's gone and hired himself a gunman,' Jack said, as he entered the bunkhouse and sat down at the table where Jed was playing poker with a few of the hands.

'That sounds ominous.'

'From the rumours doing the rounds he's hired the feller to kill you.'

'That doesn't surprise me,' Jed said without looking up from his cards. 'Did you happen to catch this gunman's name?'

'Heard somebody say he goes by the name of Brad Ryker.'

This time Jed did look up from his cards.

Jack noticed the concerned look on his friend's face. 'Do you know the feller?'

Jed nodded. 'I know him.'

'Care to tell me what you know about him?'

'He's about as cold blooded a killer as you could ever have the misfortune of coming across. He would kill anyone for anything if the price was right.'

Jack grimaced. 'And he's here for you.'

'Yep, Bassett wanted the best, and he's got him. Ryker hasn't failed to kill his man yet.'

'Maybe you should head off for Wyoming before Ryker arrives in Paradise. Nobody would blame you if you did. It just ain't worth staying here and dying for a fight that wasn't even yours in the first place.'

'I've never run from a fight in my life and I don't aim to start now,' Jed said firmly. 'If Ryker calls me out, then I'll be ready for him.'

'Then I'll stand by you as best I can, Jed.'

'Thanks, Jack. But it's me Ryker will be coming for, and so it's me who has to face him. Alone,' he said with emphasis. 'No offence, but you'd be no match for an experienced gunman like Brad Ryker.'

'No offence taken. Do you think you've got what it takes to stand up to him?'

'I don't know. I'm fast, but I just don't know if I'm fast enough to take Ryker or not. But I guess we're soon gunna find out.'

Jed lay awake on his bed in the Thorntons' ranch house long after its other occupants were fast asleep that night, wondering how it could all have come to this. On that fateful day just over four weeks ago when he had reined in his gelding on the hill overlooking Paradise he had had no idea just what the sleepy-looking town held in store for him. If he had, he would have just kept on riding until he reached the next town, despite how weary he had been. He was most likely going to lose his life in this sorry excuse for a haven,

111

and it was all down to no fault of his own. He just happened to be in the wrong place at the wrong time, and now he was going to pay the price for it. Paradise certainly wasn't the sanctuary it was billed to be, and Jed for one wished he had never set eyes on the place.

He was riding back from checking the fences between the Thornton and Bassett ranches the next day – they were cut again, courtesy of Jason Bassett's men – when Rebecca rode out to meet him on the white mare. He shook his head in disapproval at her as she brought the mare alongside his stallion. 'You shouldn't be out here, Rebecca, especially not alone.'

Her youthful face was lit up with a big smile. 'I'm not alone, Jed, I'm with you.'

'This isn't a game, Rebecca,' he said sternly. 'If Bassett's men get you I don't need to tell you what'll happen to you.'

'I was watching you from the house with the field glasses so I knew you were coming in,' she confessed. 'You're more than a match for any of Bassett's men. I'm perfectly safe if I'm with you.'

So she was even resorting to spying on him through her father's field glasses now? She really did have it bad for him.

She shot a quick sideways glance at him to gauge whether or not he really was annoyed with her for riding out to join him, and fancied she saw a softening in his features. 'I hope you've been giving my proposition some thought.'

'Of course I have. But we have to get this whole business with the Bassetts out of the way first.'

'Is this Ryker character that Jason Bassett's hired going to be a problem?'

Jed had hoped she hadn't heard about him. But someone back at the ranch must have blabbed. 'He's a dangerous man, Rebecca. He's killed a lot of men, and he's coming to Paradise to kill some more.'

'You included?'

'Me especially.'

'Because you killed Zach Bassett?'

Jed nodded. 'Jason Bassett is a very unforgiving man. He won't rest until he's sent me to Boot Hill.'

'This Ryker,' she said the name derisively, 'isn't in your league. If he tries anything with you he won't live long enough to tell the tale.'

Jed sighed. She had him up on a pedestal and that was a very dangerous thing to do. She had far more confidence in his abilities than he had in them himself. The truth was that Brad Ryker was a formidable opponent, and more likely the one to walk away from a showdown between the two. Being young and naïve, Rebecca thought the sun and the moon shone out of her hero, so she was going to be devastated if Ryker came out the victor. All her hopes and dreams would come crashing down around her, and he just prayed she would be strong enough to pick herself back up again and carry on with life.

'Martha Trethowen stopped by this morning on her way back from Paradise.'

Jed was only half listening. He had his mind on his inevitable showdown with Brad Ryker.

'She was saying that the whole town is talking about

113

how you out-gunned Zach Bassett. She said there are a lot of grateful folks in Paradise who think you're just the cat's whiskers. Zach caused a whole heap of trouble for some people, and now with him dead that trouble has stopped.'

Jed could concede the trouble from Zach may have stopped, but the trouble from Jason Bassett was only just getting started. He had the power to make their lives a whole lot more miserable than Zach ever had. Brad Ryker wouldn't just kill Jed when he turned up in Paradise. Bassett would use him to deal with anyone who had given him trouble in the past or looked likely to in the future. Yep, the good folks in town might be rejoicing now, but when that gunman stepped off the train and planted his feet firmly in Paradise they would be singing an entirely different tune.

'There was talk about offering you the job of sheriff when this is over. Paradise would be just that, with a good man like Jed Grayson keeping law and order is what they're saying.' She tossed her head and her glorious mane of black hair cascaded over her shoulders and down her back. 'But I told Martha that you being sheriff in Paradise just isn't going to happen. A sheriff's pay is nothing compared to what you would make as ramrod on the Circle D. Besides, I want you here with me, not in town where I'd hardly get to see you.'

She had it all worked out. Only she had forgotten one very important detail. She hadn't consulted Jed. Yep, she was going to be mighty crushed when he either bit the dust courtesy of one of Brad Ryker's bullets, or saddled up and rode off for Wyoming. Women were funny creatures in that respect. Always making long-term plans without finding out whether the man they had set their sights on shared those plans with them.

They were nearing the homestead now, and Rebecca just seemed to be getting more talkative the closer they got.

'I can't wait for the next dance they have in town. All those ladies' faces when I walk into the room on your arm. They're going to be green with envy. Are you a good dancer, Jed?'

'Huh?' He had been miles away.

'I said, are you a good dancer?'

'Not so's you'd notice. Never much cared for dancing as it happens, can't really see the point in it.'

'We'll soon fix that. A few lessons and you'll be footing it with the best of them.'

Jed wasn't sure that he wanted to be footing it with anyone, let alone the best of them – all that dressing up and being extra attentive towards the ladies just wasn't his cup of tea. Nope, he much preferred to relax of an evening with his cigarettes and the newspaper, or on occasion a book if one was to be had. There was nothing quite like a nice quiet evening at home after a hard day's work. Dancing, and compliments for the ladies, they were for those softer sorts of men, the ones who didn't like getting their hands dirty.

'We could even hold some dances out here,' Rebecca said with enthusiasm. 'The barn is big enough for that, and it's got a wooden floor. Most of the barns around here only have dirt ones.'

There would be no barn with a wooden floor at his

HELL IN PARADISE

uncle's ranch in Wyoming, and thank the Lord for that.
Barns there were built for animals and not dancing,
and that was all there was to it.

'Will you come into the house and have a cup of
coffee with me?' she asked, as they rode into the corral
and dismounted.

'I've still got a bit of work to do around the place
before it gets dark,' he said, hoping to fob her off so he
wouldn't have to spend any more time with her today.
The problem was, the longer he was in her company
the more he thought about her when he wasn't, and
that troubled him deeply. He couldn't afford to fall in
love with either her or Laney. His uncle's ranch beck-
oned, and he had no intention of letting that
opportunity slip away from him. His uncle had never
married, so the ranch would be his one day if he took
up Tom's offer to help him run it. Otherwise it would
end up going to one of his uncle's other nephews, and
Jed would miss out. There was no way he was going to
let any woman take the surety of owning his own ranch
away from him. The Thornton ranch would always be
Rebecca's no matter how long Jed lived there. He
would never escape from feeling he was free loading if
he were to marry her and inherit the Circle D, and he
believed Laney wasn't cut out to live on a ranch, so he
needed to keep his head where both of them were concerned.

'All right,' she said with resignation, 'I'll leave you be
for now at least. But I'm determined to spend some
time with you before the week is out, and that will be
just the two of us alone.'

116

He watched her as she headed towards the house, her shapely hips swaying from side to side in such a provocative manner that he hoped this business with the Bassetts would be over soon, because he didn't know if he would be able to resist her for much longer.

Jed looked up to see who was driving the gig that had just swept into the yard, and was surprised to see it was Laney. Although he had been doing his utmost to avoid her before he left for Wyoming he couldn't control the feeling of delight that took hold of him as she climbed down from the gig and made her way over to where he was chopping wood.

'Got you hard at work, have they?' she smiled so engagingly at him he couldn't prevent himself from smiling back.

'I have to earn my keep somehow.'

'I'm sure you've already done that several times over.'

Placing the axe down, he rubbed his sweating hands down his trousers to dry them. 'Have you got business with the Thorntons?'

'No, I'm here to see you.'

He wondered what she could possibly want to see him about. She had been decidedly out of sorts with him the last time he had bumped into her in town.

'There's a man turned up in Paradise. He's asking folks lots of questions about you.'

'A man . . . what does he look like?'

'He's about six foot, has blond hair, and he's got a small scar running through his left eyebrow. Oh, and he smokes foul-smelling cigars.'

'Brad Ryker,' Jed said simply. 'I knew he would turn up sooner or later.'

'I don't like him, Jed. He's a sinister sort of feller.'

'He's here for me, Laney.'

'Here for you. . . ?'

'He's a gunfighter that Jason Bassett has hired to kill me.'

A stab of adrenalin raced through her body. 'Then you must leave for Wyoming immediately.'

'I can't do that.'

'Why not? Won't he kill you if you don't?'

'He might . . . if I don't kill him first. But I'm not running from him. The Bassetts started something when I hit Paradise, something they shouldn't have. I'm not the sort of man you mess with and then not expect to reap trouble from. When I've got my dander up I don't let things go, and right now I've well and truly got my dander up.'

'You men are all the same,' she burst out angrily. 'You're so full of pride. It's just that kind of foolish pride that'll get you killed, Jed Grayson.'

Jed gave her a moment or two to calm down. 'I appreciate you coming out here to warn me that Ryker's arrived in Paradise, Laney. But I'll handle this in my own way without any interference from anyone else.'

'Well, what do I care if you get yourself killed,' she said with fervour. 'You're just a drifter passing through who wants no ties with anyone.'

The comment stung him just a little. It would be best

for both of them if she didn't care what happened to him. But deep inside it mattered to him that she did.

'Things have been set in motion that just can't be stopped, Laney,' he said in a softer tone, hoping to diffuse the situation a little. He didn't want her to head back to town still angry with him. This might be the last time they would ever see each other, and the time they had spent together while he convalesced meant too much to both of them for their acquaintance to end on a sour note. 'There's a part I have to play in this now whether I like it or not. I did, after all, kill young Zach Bassett.'

She moved closer to him and he caught a whiff of her perfume. It was the perfume she had worn every day she had come to visit him at Grandma Alice's while he was recovering, and it instantly brought back the happy memories of their time together. 'Only because he tried to kill you. It wasn't like *you* were the one trying to start something.'

'Jason Bassett doesn't care about that. He wants revenge against the man who killed his son, and he wants it now.'

She stepped so close to him that they were brushing up against each other, and then she placed her hand on his arm. 'Please be careful, Jed.'

Rebecca emerged from the barn at that very moment leading her mare and Jed's gelding, both saddled and ready for riding. Looking up in time to see the intimate touch she stopped dead in her tracks. Several seconds elapsed before she composed herself enough to carry on.

'I want to go riding,' she said when she had reached where they were standing, 'and Pa says I can only go if you go with me.'

Jed frowned. 'I do have a lot of wood to cut before dark, Rebecca.'

'One of the other hands can do that for you.' She glanced at Laney with disapproval. 'Aren't you one of the women who work at the Silver Dollar Saloon?' she asked coldly. It was obvious she was jealous. Her entire demeanour betrayed it.

'Yes, I am,' Laney said quietly, her pretty eyes locking on to her rival's and refusing to look away.

'And you have come out to the Circle D for what reason?'

'She's out here to see me, Rebecca,' Jed said irritably. 'Laney is a friend of mine.'

'I see.' She held out the gelding's reins to Jed to let him know the visit was over.

'I will be with you in a few minutes, Rebecca,' Jed said firmly, refusing to take the reins from her hand. He wasn't going to let her dictate to him whom he could spend time with, or when, for that matter.

Rebecca Thornton's face clouded over. Up until this moment she hadn't known she had a rival for Jed Grayson's affections, and it bothered her. The woman was beautiful, and much closer to Jed's age than Rebecca was. She didn't like the way the woman looked at Jed, either. It was the same way Rebecca had been looking at him these past few weeks, so she recognized the warning signs. This saloon girl was in love with the man she intended to marry herself.

'Wait for me around by the corral,' Jed said in a no-nonsense manner. 'I won't be long. I haven't finished talking to Laney yet.'

Rebecca Thornton had no choice but to comply. Jed Grayson wasn't a man to take orders from anyone, least of all a young woman barely out of her teens. With the greatest of reluctance at leaving the two alone she began to walk the horses in the direction of the corral.

'She is beautiful. I can see why you didn't come to visit me in town now,' Laney said sadly.

'Rebecca had nothing to do with that.'

'Didn't she?'

'No.'

'She seems to think you belong to her. It wasn't hard to see she thought I was encroaching on her territory.'

'I can't help what she thinks, Laney. Young women have a great many crazy ideas that I've never under-stood. But I can assure you that I don't belong to her, as you put it.'

'She might need some convincing of that.'

Jed sighed. 'I can do without this at the moment.'

'Then I'll leave you to your ride.'

As she turned to go Jed grabbed her by the arm. 'You sure do think poorly of me, Laney Landers,' he said in exasperation. 'I don't seem to be able to do anything right in your eyes.'

'I'm not judging you, Jed,' she said, her eyes moist-ening a little. 'I just wish you had been more honest with me. You knew I had fallen for you, so you should have just told me your heart was somewhere else. I wouldn't have bothered you then.'

'For crying out loud, Laney, there's nothing going on between Rebecca and me.'

Her green eyes oozed scepticism.

'And what's more, you have never been a bother to me. I enjoy your company much more than I have ever enjoyed any woman's.'

A sob burst up from somewhere deep in her chest, and without warning she turned and scurried back to the gig. She was in the seat and flicking the reins before Jed had time to cross the yard and stop her.

'Dang women,' he muttered angrily as he watched the gig rattle past the barn. 'I ain't ever going to understand 'em.'

CHAPTER THIRTEEN

Jed reached for the Winchester he kept beside him at all times the moment he heard the thundering of horses' hoofs sweeping down the slope towards the Thornton homestead. If he wasn't very much mistaken it would be Jason Bassett and his men. Leaving the saddle he had been mending on the corral fence, he quickly made his way over to the front veranda of the ranch house, and with a lump forming in his throat, waited for the horsemen to arrive.

Thomas Thornton stepped out the front door with a scattergun in his hand, and hard on his heels was Jack, a six-gun held at the ready in each hand.

Jed glanced around the yard. One of the hands who had been forking hay in the loft had abandoned his pitchfork and was crouching in the open window with a Colt Peacemaker nestled in his palm. The window of an upstairs room flew up and a double-barrel shotgun made its appearance. Rebecca Thornton was determined to protect her man.

Eight horses slid to a halt beneath the steps leading

up to the veranda, all snorting loudly, and with manes and tails flicking they pranced up and down on the spot as their riders attempted to bring them under control.

'What do you want, Bassett?' Thomas Thornton demanded.

'You know what I want, Thornton,' Bassett said angrily. 'I want the man who killed my boy.'

Jed stepped forward. 'Then I'm the feller you're looking for.' His hand rested lightly beside his Navy Colt in expectation.

Jason Bassett stabbed a stubby finger in Jed's direction. 'You go get your horse. You're coming with us.'

'No he isn't,' Thornton said firmly. 'Jed's a Circle D man and everyone on this ranch stands behind him.'

'Then you're all gunna die!'

Jed's eyes quickly ran over Bassett. With bloated face and body from years of excess, his red face was even redder from the exertion of the fast ride out to the Circle D Ranch, and his darting eyes told Jed he was a man given to his fair share of paranoia. Brad Ryker was easy to pick out. Sitting ramrod straight in the saddle, he displayed a certain grace that let all and sundry know he was extremely confident. His gun hand rested on his thigh inches away from the butt of his Remington, and his grey eyes were scrutinizing Jed with profound intensity.

'Nobody is gunna die today,' Jed said calmly. 'Not unless you try something stupid. Best you look around you a little. I think you'll find we've got plenty of guns trained on you and your men.'

Those darting eyes did the rounds of the barnyard,

taking in the shotgun in the window and the one in the loft. One of Thornton's men had even materialized over at the corral and had a Winchester pointed straight at the bunch.

'Now you see what you're up against.'

'You killed my boy in cold blood,' Bassett rasped.

'He had it coming.'

'He was no gunfighter!'

'Nope, he wasn't,' Jed agreed. 'He was a lowdown dirty back-shooter.'

Jason Bassett's body stiffened right there in the saddle. Nobody spoke about his son like that and got away with it. He jerked his thumb in Ryker's direction. 'Do you know who this feller is?' he asked gruffly.

'Yep, he's a cold-blooded killer who hires himself out to scum who are too cowardly to do their own dirty work.'

Bassett slowly shook his head at him. 'Oh, I'm gunna enjoy watching you die.'

'If I do die I'm sure it won't be you pulling the trigger.'

'You're an insolent punk, Grayson. But all the insolence in the world ain't gunna save you this time.'

'Make your play then, Bassett, and we'll see which of us comes out on top.'

Jason Bassett glanced at Ryker, who shook his head. He had seen the guns trained on them and realized it would be suicide to try anything now. Better to wait for a more opportune time.

'My boy didn't deserve what you did to him,' Bassett snarled. 'His life was just beginning. Everything I've

125

worked so hard to build up all these years I did for him.
Now it's all for nothing.'

'Your son was a spoilt bully who terrorized the citizens of Paradise. If you'd been man enough to rein him
in then he wouldn't be six feet under right now. You're
to blame for what happened to him.'

'Don't you dare try to place the blame on me, you
filthy gutter rat! We were doing fine until you breezed
into Paradise.'

'Until I breezed into Paradise, as you put it, everyone
was too scared to stand up to that sorry excuse for the
man you called your son. It was having me stand up to
him that he couldn't handle. That's why he jumped me
and beat me up, that's why he tried to back-shoot me,
and that's why he lost his life.'

Bassett couldn't control his rage any more, and so his
hand closed over the butt of his pistol.

'You go right ahead,' Jed said totally unflustered.
'Reach for that shooting iron and let me send another
Bassett to Boot Hill.'

'I think we should leave it for now, Mr Bassett,' Ryker
said quickly, and not without a certain amount of
anxiety that his employer might do something fool-
hardy that would get them all killed.

'What am I paying you for?' Bassett snarled, twisting
in the saddle to glare at the man who had dared to give
him advice.

'Now is not the time, Mr Bassett. That time will
come, I give you my word on that. But not right now.'

As quickly as Jason Bassett's fury had blown up, it then
subsided. 'I'll bow to your judgement on this occasion,

Ryker,' he said reluctantly, and then turned his attention back to Jed. 'Your day is coming, you saddle tramp. No one harms a Bassett and lives to tell his kids about it. You'll be dead before the week is out.'

'Maybe, but then again, maybe not – I guess it'll all come down to whether or not your hired help can take me.'

Ryker grinned down at Jed from his lofty position astride his mount. 'I doubt you'll present me with any problems, sidewinder.'

Jed stepped clear of the overhang of the verandah roof and into the sunshine. 'Care to try me right now, then, Ryker?'

The grin on Brad Ryker's face faded immediately. He had never been challenged before. It was always him doing the challenging. This was something he wasn't used to, and for a moment it threw him.

'Cat got your tongue, big man?'

Being the professional he was, Ryker recovered from the shock quickly. 'We'll square off when I'm good and ready,' he said without a hint of fear. 'Not when you decide, and definitely not when you've got so many guns pointed in my direction. I'm not interested in anything that isn't a fair fight.'

'That's not what I've heard.'

For the first time Ryker's face displayed his annoyance. 'Nobody can accuse me of being a back-shooter. When I come for you you'll know about it in advance.'

'I can hardly wait,' Jed said, his voice dripping with sarcasm.

'Let's ride,' Jason Bassett said suddenly, obviously

bored with mere talking instead of action being taken. He wheeled his horse around and was halfway out of the yard before his men had even put spurs to their mounts.

'That Ryker's one mean-looking hombre,' Jack said, as he stepped forward to stand beside Jed and stare after the retreating backs of Jason Bassett and his men.

'You don't know the half of it, Jack,' Jed said, his attention focused on the tall form of the gunfighter as it bobbed expertly up and down on his custom-made saddle. 'He's one man who doesn't deserve to be walking God's green earth, given some of the things he has done.'

Jack looked at Jed, allowing the faintest of smiles to flicker across his lips. 'Time he wasn't, then.'

'I'll give the job of seeing he doesn't to you, if you feel that strongly about it.'

'And steal your thunder? I wouldn't dream of it.'

A grin lit up Jed's face this time. 'Somehow I figured that would be your answer.'

Jason Bassett stepped up his persecution of the Thorntons over the next few days. Fences were cut and Circle D cattle driven across the boundary to be mixed in with Bassett's own herd, and Jack came across several dead steers at a waterhole that Bassett's men had obviously poisoned. Something had to be done, and it had to be done quickly, or else the Circle D Ranch would go bust.

Jack crossed the yard one morning to speak to Jed as he sat on the front steps of the Thorntons' homestead smoking a cigarette. 'Mr Thornton wants me and the hands to cross over on to Bassett's land, and cut out the Circle D beef and bring it home,' he said, sitting down beside Jed and beginning the process of rolling his own cigarette. 'Bassett's driven off over five hundred head this time.'

'That's likely to cost lives,' Jed said quietly.

'Neither he nor I can think of any other way of getting those cattle back, Jed.'

Jed thought it over. Bassett would change the brands on those cattle and sell them at the first chance he got. If Thornton was to get them back he would have to do something pretty reckless or kiss goodbye to that beef forever. 'I'll come with you if you want me to,' he said eventually.

'I was hoping you would. I don't think we can do this without you being with us.'

'They will most likely have driven those cattle close to the Bassett homestead. That means they probably haven't had time to use a running iron on them to change the brand yet. If we head off straightaway we just might catch them in the act.'

'Catching them in the act won't prevent them from trying to stop us taking those cattle back,' Jack pointed out.

'Maybe not. But at least it'll mean we're only trying to take what's ours, and not disputed cattle. I'd feel a whole lot better about using my gun then, if it came down to it.'

Taking a few more draws on his smoke and then flicking what remained of it into the bushes beside the front steps, Jack stood up and, with a deep sigh, set his face towards the corral. 'I'll go and get the boys together. We'll ride as soon as the horses are saddled.'

Jed made his way back up to his bedroom to fetch his guns. He would take his Navy Colt of course, and the better of his two Winchesters. He bumped into Rebecca on the landing as he was leaving the room.

'Are you going to bring the cattle back?' she asked, looking at the weapons he held in his hands.

'I'm afraid we've got no choice but to, Rebecca.'

'Oh, Jed, please be careful,' she said anxiously. 'If anything happened to you I'd . . .' she couldn't bring herself to finish the sentence, instead, a tear rolled down her cheek, followed by another, and then another, until they had become a veritable flood.

'It'll be all right,' he said unconvincingly, and then placed a hand on her shoulder in a futile attempt to comfort her.

Rebecca Thornton snuggled into him with her entire body, and he couldn't say that he didn't like it; she was about as shapely as a woman could get, and the effect of having her flesh pressed hard against him was about the most pleasant thing a man could ever experience.

'Promise me you won't try to be a hero if Jason Bassett's men turn up,' she implored him, as she looked up into his face from her tear-drenched eyes.

'I won't do anything stupid, if that's what you're worried about.'

She knew that was about as close to a promise as she was going to get. A man like Jed Grayson didn't shy away from a fight if one came his way. She just hoped that if one did, he would have what it took to come out on top.

'I have to go and saddle up my horse,' he said gently, when after a few minutes she still hadn't let go of him. 'I mustn't keep the others waiting.'

She reluctantly pulled away and stood before him, looking about as forlorn as a woman could when the man she loved was going off to risk his life.

'Make sure you stay right here with your pa until we get back,' he said firmly. 'Don't try to follow. There's nothing you can do to help, but if they got a hold of you, you'd end up wishing you'd never been born.'

Rebecca had secretly planned to follow behind at a distance. She wasn't a bad shot with a rifle, so if Jed got into any sort of trouble she might be able to save him.

'I mean it, Rebecca,' he said sternly. It was almost as if he had read her mind. 'I know you only too well now, and your impulsiveness would get you into trouble this time.'

'I'll stay behind, if that's what you want me to do,' she said in an uncharacteristically submissive manner.

'If you got hurt on account of me I'd never forgive myself. So yes, I do want you to stay here.'

She looked pleased by what he had just said, and suddenly going up on tiptoe, kissed him on the lips. 'I'll be praying for you,' she said, then she turned and walked swiftly across the landing and down the stairs.

Jack had the horses saddled by the time he reached the corral. 'Ready?' he asked Jed, as the man who had become his friend opened the corral gate.

'Ready as I'll ever be, Jack.'

131

Jack Wilson waited patiently as Jed climbed into the saddle of his gelding and seated himself comfortably. If they were going to be successful, then he knew everything would hinge on Jed's abilities with a six-gun when they reached the Bassett ranch.

'Let's go get these cattle back,' Jed said as he gave the gelding a nudge, and holding the reins loosely in one hand rode him out of the corral and towards the range beyond the house that would take them to the Bassett ranch.

Jed thought about the task ahead as he and Jack rode along side by side without saying a word to each other. This could be the last time he ever looked up at that vast expanse of blue sky that covered his world overhead. The sky that he had taken for granted so many times in the past, but which now struck him so powerfully with its beauty. Was this the last time he would ride the range and feel the warmth of the sun on his back and have the gentle breeze caress his face, or sleep out beneath the myriad of stars that illuminated the night sky? Why did it take the threat of death to make a man appreciate what the good Lord had so freely given to him?

Jed suddenly realized he had forgotten to wire his uncle and let him know he might not make it to Wyoming. The poor old fellow would be sick with worry if Jed didn't turn up and he hadn't heard word as to why not. He hadn't even told anyone his uncle's name, let alone how to get in touch with him if he were to die. He felt bad about it, but there was nothing he could do about it now.

An hour later they rode through the cut fence, its posts ripped out of the ground for a distance of about a hundred yards, barbed wire snipped in more places than Jed cared to count. Bassett had done a thorough job of opening up the Thornton range to his own cattle.

Just over the fence on Bassett land Jack Wilson called a halt, and turning around in the saddle he addressed the six men following closely behind him. 'If any of you want to pull out and head back to the Circle D, now's the time to do it. Neither Mr Thornton nor I will hold it against you. We don't have the right to ask you to risk your lives as it is.'

Six heads shook almost in unison.

'God bless each and every one of you then,' Jack said sincerely, 'and may you come through this unscathed.'

The party of men continued on without speaking, each one lost in his own thoughts on what fate might have in store for them just up ahead. If any of them was frightened then he wasn't showing any signs of it.

A mile out from the Bassett homestead they crested a rise and looked down on a wide and lush valley, well watered and stocked with cattle.

'I'm willing to bet that herd over by the river is Circle D beef,' Jack said, pointing towards a grouping of cattle being herded into a tight bunch beside a bend of the slow-flowing watercourse.

Jed pulled his field glasses out of his saddlebags, and putting them to his eyes, carefully studied the activity down by the river. 'They're pulling them down three at a time and branding them,' he said as he handed the glasses to Jack.

'I make it ten men,' Jack said before passing them back to Jed.

Jed nodded. 'Eight of us and ten of them – I reckon that's much better odds than I was expecting.'

'Let's mosey on down and make our presence felt,' Jack said, urging his horse down the slope and beckoning to his men to follow as he did so.

Jed wondered how long it would be before one of Bassett's men spotted them approaching and raised the alarm. The closer they could get to those cattle before anyone knew they were in the vicinity, the easier things would go for them.

So engrossed were they in the task of roping steers and branding them, Jason Bassett's hands didn't notice the Circle D men until they were a mere three hundred yards distant. But the shout that went up from the one who did spot them was enough to drown out the lowing of cattle, and informed his comrades that trouble was at hand.

Every single one of Bassett's men dropped what they were doing and rallied to face the sudden threat. By the time Jed and his small band had reached the cattle, Bassett's men had formed a tight defensive group, their firearms at the ready.

Jed was at once surprised to see Jason Bassett amongst their number, and then relieved to see that Brad Ryker was not.

'What are you men doing on my land?' Bassett barked furiously when they were within earshot.

'Let me do the talking, Jack,' Jed said as they

approached cautiously.

'Whatever you think is best, Jed.'

Jed waited until he was within easy speaking distance before he answered. Besides, he wanted to make absolutely sure they were Circle D cattle that Bassett and his men were passing a running iron over before he started flinging around the accusations. Yep, he passed one . . . two . . . and now three steers with the Circle D brand clearly stamped on their rumps. Jason Bassett was definitely engaging in an act of rustling.

'I won't ask you again,' Bassett roared. 'Tell me what you're doing on my land, or I'll send lead flying in your direction.'

'We're here to take back what rightfully belongs to Thomas Thornton, and if you start shooting it'll be the last thing you or any of your men ever do,' Jed said ferociously.

Bassett noted the weapons clutched in the hands of the men from the Circle D Ranch and decided to adopt a cautious approach. 'There aren't any cattle belonging to the Circle D on this ranch.'

Jed moved his gelding clear of Jack and the rest of Thornton's men, and over to where Jason Bassett was standing, and glared down at him. 'You're lying through your back teeth, Bassett. I've just ridden past three steers with the Circle D brand on their rumps.'

'A few of Thornton's cattle might have wandered through the boundary fence,' Bassett said defensively.

'The boundary fence that you ordered your men to cut. And what's that you're holding in your hand? It looks mighty like a running iron to me. Touching up a

135

few of the brands, are you?'

'If I want to use a running iron on my cattle, then that's my business,' Bassett said angrily.

'Ah, but you're not using it on your own cattle, are you, Bassett? You're using it to change the brand on Circle D beef.'

'That's a damnable lie!'

Slipping off his gelding's back Jed wandered over to where three of Bassett's men were holding a steer down next to the fire, and looked down at the animal's rump. 'That looks mighty like a Circle D brand to me, and that red-hot running iron you're holding in your hand is fresh out of the fire.' He glanced all around as if he were looking for something. 'I can't see any other cattle close enough for you to be thinking of branding, so I figure it must be this one you were about to work on before we interrupted you.'

'You think you're so clever, don't you, Grayson? Well, if Ryker was here, he'd wipe that smug look off your face for you.'

'Just where is that lapdog of yours, Bassett?'

'Not that it's any business of yours, but I sent him into town on an errand for me.'

'Now that wasn't the smartest of things to do, was it? Without him around you've got no chance of stopping us from taking back what rightfully belongs to Thomas Thornton.'

Jason Bassett eyed him coldly. 'We'll see about that.'

More of Bassett's men were leaving the herd and drifting in to see what was going on.

'You all right, Mr Bassett?' one of them asked as he

dismounted from a bay mare and walked over to where his boss was standing.

'Nope, this feller and his pack of dogs reckon they're gunna take the herd off us.'

'Me and the boys ain't gunna let them do that to you, Mr Bassett.'

'Thank you, Clint; I knew I could count on you.'

Jed eyeballed Clint with disdain. 'Are you telling me that even though you know these cattle have been stolen from the Thornton family, you would fight to prevent us from reclaiming them?'

'I stand where Mr Bassett stands. If he says the cattle stay here, then I'll dang well make sure they do.'

'Then I'll dang well make sure you're the first feller I shoot when someone tries to stop us,' Jed said with passion. 'If there's one thing I hate it's a polecat that rustles another man's beef and then fights to keep it when he's been caught red-handed with it.'

'Enough talk, Grayson,' Bassett said, his confidence returning now that his men were turning up and lending him their support. 'I want you and Wilson, and the others riding with you, off my ranch right now!'

Jed turned round and nodded to Jack. 'Round up Mr Thornton's cattle, and shoot anyone who tries to stop you.'

As Jack wheeled his horse around to carry out the directive, Clint went for his six-gun to stop him. As quick as a flash Jed's Navy Colt sprang into his hand and exploded into life, a lump of hot lead hitting the hapless cowboy just below the breastbone and ending any hopes he had of currying favour with his employer.

Jason Bassett had gone for his gun a split second after his top hand, and although he had the Remington clear of the holster and pointed in Jed's direction he never got to pull the trigger. A second bullet from Jed's pistol tore through his chest, nicking his heart before cutting a savage pathway out of his back. Dropping the six-gun, he lurched forwards with a look of disbelief on his face – it was as if he couldn't believe that the moment of his death had arrived. Then with blood spilling from the wound at a rapid pace, he sank first to his knees, and then as he became weaker from the loss of blood, lay quietly face down on the soil of his own ranch and died.

'Your boss is dead, so nobody else needs to die,' Jed yelled out quickly, hoping to avert any more bloodshed. 'All we want to do is take back what rightfully belongs to Thomas Thornton.'

'Come on, boys,' one of Bassett's men said suddenly, 'we're out of a job now, so let's leave them to it. There's nothing to be gained by shooting it out now that Mr Bassett's dead.'

Jed kept his Navy Colt in his hand until they had ridden off in the direction of the homestead, hopefully to gather up what few belongings they had and head off to who knows where looking for another ranch to work on.

Slipping his six-gun back in its holster, Jed swung himself back up on his horse. 'Let's take Mr Thornton's cattle back to him and tell him his trouble with the Bassetts is over for good, Jack.'

CHAPTER FOURTEEN

Jed knew she would broach the subject again, especially now that the conflict with the Bassetts was over and she knew Jed would be heading for Wyoming real soon. He allowed her to take him on a picnic at a bend in the river on the Circle D Ranch that she was particularly fond of. He had practised what he would say long and hard, so when the moment came he was ready for it.

'Jed, the time has come for you to give me your answer to the question I asked you a while back,' she began nervously. 'I am yours for the taking if you want me. I hope you have done what you promised me you would, and given it plenty of thought.' She had chosen to wear the tightest pair of riding breeches that accentuated her curvy hips, and Jed couldn't help noticing she had left the top few buttons on her blouse undone, which displayed her more than ample cleavage. Rebecca Thornton wasn't leaving anything to chance. She was going to make it as difficult as she possibly could for Jed to turn her down by showing him what he would be forfeiting if he did.

Putting down his piece of fried chicken, Jed cleared his throat before beginning. 'I'm flattered that you want me to marry you, Rebecca, and I have given the proposal more thought than you could believe possible these past few days, believe me I have. But I don't feel that my future lies on the Circle D – my future is on my uncle's ranch in Wyoming.'

She looked crestfallen. 'But the Circle D can offer you so much more. There is room for us to expand now that the Bassetts are no longer a threat. You could end up owning the biggest ranch in the territory.'

'The Thorntons could end up owning the biggest ranch in the territory,' he corrected her.

'But if you married me you would become a Thorn . . .' she stopped, realizing what it was she was saying.

'And therein lies the problem, Rebecca. You see, I'm not a Thornton and never will be. I'm a Grayson, and I'm proud to be one. My uncle is a Grayson, and so his ranch is Grayson land. That's where my heart is, and where I belong.'

'What can I do to change your mind?' she asked desperately.

'Marry me and come and live with me on Grayson land,' he said quietly, already knowing what her answer would be, but determined to get her to see where he was coming from.

'I can't do that, I belong here,' she said suddenly, looking at him as if the suggestion he had made was the

140

craziest thing she had ever heard. Then her shoulders slumped. 'Yes, I see your point. I was expecting you to do something I am not prepared to do myself.'

'I would always feel that I was an intruder here, Rebecca. That I should be taking orders from you because it was really your land.'

'I would never do that to you,' she insisted. 'But I can see how you might feel that way.'

'I do like you, and you wouldn't be hard to love, it's just that we each belong somewhere else, and to take one of us away from where we really belong would cause both of us a lot of pain in the long run.'

She nodded, although he could see she was terribly disappointed.

Jed smiled tenderly at her. 'You will meet someone one day who will make you wonder what you ever saw in me.'

'I'm in love with you, Jed, so it's hard for me to believe that will ever be possible right now.'

'You will, you'll see. And I'll be back this way some time, and I'll call in and see how you're doing. You'll most likely have a few kids by then.'

'And so will you, too,' she said morosely, 'and I'll be green with envy that they aren't the children I'd had with you. She will be a lucky woman who gets your wedding ring on her finger, Jed Grayson.'

Jed figured it would be unlikely he would ever get married at all. It would have to be a remarkable woman who agreed to a life of deprivation on a small ranch that required surviving the harshness of a Wyoming winter, and he doubted such a woman could be found.

Jed said his goodbyes to the Thorntons and the hands of the Circle D Ranch the next morning; then mounting his faithful gelding, he rode out of the yard and up the slope towards the road that would take him to Paradise. He would spend a night at Grandma Alice's, say his farewell to Laney Landers, share a final drink with Jack Wilson at the Golden Nugget Saloon, and then head off to his future in Wyoming, probably never to return this way again.

As Jed rode towards the town that had almost cost him his life it was a hot day with a sky so blue that it almost made a man's heart sing with the beauty of it. He couldn't say he would be recommending Paradise to anyone as the sort of town that lived up to its name, but at least he would be leaving it alive, and only a few days back that was something he had doubted would happen – so at least that was something to be grateful for.

A few hours later he discovered that the main street of Paradise was just as dry as it was the last time he had guided his horse along it, and the dust that swirled up from its hard surface tickled his nostrils and scratched the back of his throat in much the same manner it had on that occasion as well. Yep, the township of Paradise didn't have too much to recommend it at all, and Jed figured it wouldn't tug at his heartstrings overly much to leave it behind when the time came to move on.

'So you've come back, then,' Grandma Alice said when she opened the door to his knock and saw him standing there.

He grinned at her. 'I just couldn't stay away from the

142

prettiest woman in the whole of Paradise, Alice.'

'Get away with you,' she said waving her hand at him in embarrassment. 'You're a sweet talker if ever I did meet one.'

'I need a room just for tonight if you can put me up, Alice.'

'I always have a room for you, Jed Grayson,' she said as she ushered him through the door. 'I hear you fixed Jason Bassett's wick a couple of days back. The whole town's talking about it. Now maybe things in Paradise can get back to how they used to be before Bassett ruined the place.'

'I hope so, Alice, I sincerely hope so.'

Stopping midway up the stairs she turned and looked down at him with her aged but still lively blue eyes. 'You aren't planning on putting down roots here in Paradise, are you? I'll let you have your room for next to nothing if you do. Just do a few chores for me now and again and we'll call it even.'

Jed shook his head. 'I'm afraid not, Alice. Wyoming's been calling to me mighty strong just of late. I reckon I'll head off in that direction in a day or two.'

'Shame, I'd got used to seeing you around town of late.' She hesitated and he picked up on it.

'Spit it out, Alice, there's something on your mind, and if you don't let it out I'll reckon you'll be fit to burst.'

She smiled at his comment. 'You read me too well, young feller.'

'Let's have it then.'

'It's just that I was kinda hoping you'd stick around

for the Landers gal. She's a sweet little thing and I got to be quite fond of her when she was coming here every day to visit you while you were laid up. I think she's gunna be mighty disappointed to see you leave Paradise.'

'We're cut from different cloth, Laney and me are, Alice. I don't reckon she'd take to ranch life too well, and I'd be hopeless living in town. What would I do for a job, anyhow?'

'I think you might be doing that gal a disservice, Jed Grayson. She'd make a fine wife, and I reckon she'd take to ranch life like a duck to water, given half a chance.'

Jed couldn't see it, but didn't wish to belabour the point. Instead he just nodded, letting Alice know the conversation with regard to Miss Laney Landers was over, and then followed her upstairs to the little room at the end of the landing.

Jed almost walked smack bang into him as he was coming out of the mercantile, and the shock of seeing him left him bereft of the powers of speech for a moment.

'Heard you laid Jason Bassett in the dust the other day,' Brad Ryker said, an evil grin tilting up the corner of his mouth just enough to reveal his tobacco-stained teeth. He patted the breast pocket of his shirt. 'I'm glad the old buzzard paid me before you dealt to him or I wouldn't be too pleased with you right about now. And that wouldn't have done your long-term health any good at all.'

144

'What are you still doing in Paradise, Ryker?' Jed asked, finally finding his tongue would work after all.

'With all this money burning a hole in my pocket I decided to spend some of it in Paradise before I head off. Figure I might try Abilene next and see what kinda luck that brings me.'

'If you keep living by that shooting iron of yours then your luck's gunna run out much sooner than you think.'

Brad Ryker laughed. 'It ain't run out yet, and I don't expect it to for a long while to come.' His gun hand tapped the side of his holster. 'This thing will make sure of that.'

'Pride goeth before a fall, Ryker; you'd do well to remember that.'

But Ryker wasn't listening: he was looking at something over Jed's shoulder, something that held his interest too much for him to be taking in what Jed was saying. Jed turned to see what it could be that was so beguiling him.

Laney Landers was moving down the boardwalk towards them with all the grace and natural sensuality she possessed in abundance, and as Jed watched her approach he couldn't say he blamed Ryker for being spellbound: she was a beauty in any man's book.

'Well, I *am* in Paradise, so I reckon I've just seen my first angel,' Ryker said with enthusiasm.

'I'm so glad you're all right, Jed,' Laney said when she had reached them. 'When I heard there had been trouble out at the Bassett ranch the other day I feared for the worst. But then someone told me you were safe, and I was so relieved.'

Brad Ryker didn't say a word, but just stood there open-mouthed and taking in every inch of the delight-ful creature.

'I'm fine, Laney,' Jed said, his heart beating a little faster at the sight of her. Not having seen her for a while he had almost forgotten how stunning she really was.

'You were going to say goodbye to me before you headed off weren't you?'

He nodded. 'Of course, that's the main reason I stopped off in Paradise.'

The faintest of smiles flickered across her face. 'I wish you would stay in Paradise, Jed.'

'My uncle's ranch has too big a hold on me I'm afraid, Laney.'

'It's a good dream to have, Jed, and I wish you all the best in it.' Placing her hands on his shoulders she tilted up her face and kissed him lightly on the lips, before brushing past and continuing on down the boardwalk so he wouldn't see the tears that were beginning to flood her green eyes.

'Well, I'll be . . .' Ryker said, pushing his Stetson clear of his forehead so he could get a better view of her disappearing form. 'That's one little lady I'd be only too happy to get to know.'

'Too bad you're heading for Abilene, then.'

'Maybe I'll hang around in Paradise for a bit longer than I intended.'

'So long, Ryker,' Jed said with cold indifference as he stepped around the man, 'I hope we never meet again.'

CHAPTER FIFTEEN

Jed was waiting at the bar that afternoon for Jack Wilson to turn up for his farewell drink when the Thorntons' foreman walked in with a worried look dominating his features.

'Something's up, I can tell by the look on your face,' Jed said as Jack joined him at the bar.

'I'm sorry to be the one to tell you this, Jed, 'cos I know how much you like her, but Laney Landers has been attacked.'

Jed stared at him as if he hadn't heard what he had said.

'She's over at Doc Holland's at the moment. I found her in the alley between Lars Sorenson's Mercantile and that Chinese laundry.'

Jed's normally tanned face went as white as a sheet. 'Who did it to her?'

'She told me it was Brad Ryker. He dragged her off the boardwalk and down the alley. She fought hard, but he's a big strong man, Jed.'

'Did he. . . ?'

'No, thank the Lord. Me and some of the boys from the Circle D were walking past and heard her scream. Ryker ran off when he saw us enter the alley with our shooting irons at the ready.' He paused just long enough for Jed to take in the information. 'He knocked her around purdy bad, though. Fair laid into her with his fists to try and subdue her, from what I can gather. Doc Holland says she's most likely got a couple of cracked ribs.'

Jed's mind raced. Ryker would try it again. There was no one in town willing to take him on in a gunfight, and that was the only thing that would stop him from getting at Laney again. He was one ruthless piece of trash, that was for certain. If Laney was to be safe from him after Jed had left Paradise, then Ryker would have to be stopped for good.

'Where is Ryker now?'

'I saw him go into the Silver Dollar not more than fifteen minutes ago.' He looked intently at Jed's determined face. 'You're not thinking of going up against him are you?'

'Somebody has to, or there's no telling how many women he'll harm.'

'But you're no match for Brad Ryker. You'd just be signing your own death warrant if you're foolish enough to call him out.'

'I'm not gunna leave Laney unprotected.'

'She will be if you're dead. There'd be nothing to stop Ryker then. The boys and I can't be around to watch over her every minute of the day. We've got a ranch to run.'

148

'All the more reason for me to step up and do the job myself,' Jed said firmly. 'I need you to tell Ryker I want to meet him out in the street in half an hour.'

'And what if he refuses?'

'Tell him that Jed Grayson reckons he's a lily-livered coward who's no match for a real man, and if he isn't out in that street ready to face me in half an hour then I'll come into the saloon and drag him out kicking and screaming like the frightened little boy that he is.'

'I reckon that'll bring him out looking to fix your wick,' Jack conceded. 'I just hope he doesn't decide to shoot the messenger before he does.'

Jed headed for the street in front of Sorenson's Mercantile and Chang's Laundry. When he cut Ryker down he wanted it to be beside the alley where he had so cruelly attacked Laney. As he planted his feet in the dusty street, the hot sun shining directly overhead, he fed a couple of shells into his Navy Colt, then slipping it back into his holster, waited patiently for the man he now hated to make his appearance.

It was ironic really. The name Paradise evoked an image of a tranquil setting, a place where peace reigned supreme, and men, women and children lived in harmony side by side. But the Paradise in which he stood now bore little resemblance to that illusion: men of the ilk of Brad Ryker and the Bassetts had made it hell in Paradise, and now not only was its main street about to echo to the sound of six-guns, it was about to run red with the blood of a man as well.

Jed pulled his fob watch from the pocket of his trousers and checked the time. Ryker had only five minutes left to make his appearance before Jed must make good his threat and go down to the Silver Dollar and drag him out. He wondered what he would do if he pushed his way through those batwings and found the man gone – slipped out the back and now far away from the showdown he had been challenged to. Would he go after him? He was angry enough to. He felt his pulse quicken merely at the thought of what that man had done to Laney, and what he *would* have done to her if Jack hadn't happened along when he did. That answered his question for him. He would go after him because he couldn't rest until he had made him pay.

He realized he must have feelings for the woman after all. He had suspected he had all along, but not until this moment had he realized just how strong those feelings really were. He had suppressed them because of the fear that Laney would do to him what Belinda had done, and he dreaded that more than he dreaded copping a slug from Brad Ryker's six-gun.

One minute to go, and so Jed slipped the fob watch back in his pocket and bit down gently on his bottom lip in apprehension as he stared at the batwings of the Silver Dollar Saloon, half hoping they would open and Ryker would emerge, and half hoping he had already left Paradise far behind.

With barely seconds to go those batwings parted company and Brad Ryker stepped confidently out on to the boardwalk, gazing up the street towards where Jed stood rooted to the spot, determined to see this thing through to the bitter end.

Jed's heart skipped a beat. Ryker looked tall and

impressive, clad from head to toe in black: a more sin-
ister-looking adversary a man could never expect to
come up against. For a second or two Jed contemplated
turning and skedaddling just as fast as his legs would
carry him. What had he been thinking when he issued
this crazy challenge to the man who had put so many
others in their grave, and was likely within the next few
minutes to put Jed in his?

Ryker plucked a half-smoked cigarette from between
his lips, flicking it without any fanfare on to the dried
mud in front of the boardwalk; then with a casualness
that spoke of his total disrespect for his challenger's
ability with a six-gun, stepped down off the boardwalk
to begin his advance up the street.

Jed swallowed down the hard lump that had formed
in his throat, but it merely sprang back up again. It was
his hand that troubled him the most, however: it just
wouldn't stop shaking, and he knew that if he couldn't
bring it under control by the time Ryker reached him,
then he wouldn't have a snowball's chance in hell of
beating the hired killer to the draw.

Ryker had sauntered a good thirty yards now, and Jed
was able to see the sun glinting off the silver butt of his
six-gun as it swayed slightly with every step he took.
Brad Ryker looked the consummate professional, and
Jed wondered what he looked like to the man
approaching him. Did Jed look like a man at the top of
his game, confidence oozing from every pore? Or did
he look like just another wannabe cowpoke that Ryker
was confident he could beat?

Jed's question was answered when he realized that

Ryker's pace hadn't slackened, nor had it quickened. It was a leisurely advance that told him the man considered this contest to be nothing more than another notch on his gun.

Twenty more yards and Jed could see the expression on the gunfighter's face. Hard as granite: not a muscle so much as twitched, Brad Ryker was all determination. Ten yards further on he stopped and stared straight at Jed for a moment before speaking.

'You made the biggest mistake of your life, calling me out like this. I was all for leaving Paradise in a few days' time and forgetting about how you challenged me that day out at the Thorntons'. But sending your messenger boy into the Silver Dollar with your insults made me change my mind. I'm gunna enjoy slinging my lead through you, Grayson, and then I'm gunna rope your mangy carcase and drag it behind my stallion the entire length of Paradise.'

Jed was surprised to discover that now the man was standing in front of him the lump in his throat and the shaking hand had disappeared, and so too had the fear.

'I suspect you've never had to draw on someone who knows how to handle a gun, Ryker. It'd mostly be cowpokes and sodbusters. Well, you're about to face your first test, and you'd better be every bit as fast as you boast you are, because if you ain't I'm gunna be sending you up to sleep on Boot Hill tonight, and every night from now on until the second coming.'

'You talk mighty big, Grayson. But I ain't never heard no talk of you ever gunning any big names down.

You're way out of your depth, and what's more, you know it.'

'I wouldn't have called you out at all if you hadn't done what you did to Laney. But a man like you doesn't deserve to live who would treat a woman like that.'

A light went on in Ryker's head. 'So that's what this is all about! You have a fancy for the little dance-hall gal.' He chuckled. 'Well, after I've dealt to you, I'm gunna finish what I started with that little green-eyed beauty, yes sirree, I am. I was only getting started when I got interrupted.'

'You ran like a frightened rabbit was the way I heard it.' Jed noticed the cut running down the entire length of Ryker's left cheek. 'Looks to me like Laney gave you back as good as she got. That cheek of yours has been bleeding like a stuck pig.'

Brad Ryker's eyebrows came down slightly in annoyance. 'If she'd just kept still I wouldn't have had to belt her so much. The stupid little cow was biting and scratching so much I had no choice.'

'You had the choice not to touch her in the first place,' Jed countered angrily. 'You're a sorry excuse for a man, if ever I've seen one. But after today you won't be bothering a woman ever again.'

'I'll take any woman I have a mind to take,' Ryker said resolutely. 'But you won't be alive to see it.'

'I'm done with talking, Ryker. Why don't you just make a play for that fancy shooting iron of yours and get this whole business over with? I've got other things I want to do with the rest of my day.'

'You're a cocky rooster, Grayson, but that'll be your undoing. Say your prayers, cos I'm about to send you straight to hell.'

Jed's gun hand was resting just to the side of his holster, a mere inch away from the butt of the Navy Colt that nestled comfortably there. When Ryker made his move he would be ready for him.

Jed noticed Ryker had a nervous habit: his left eyelid would flutter rapidly every now and again, indicating to Jed that there might just be the smallest shadow of a doubt in the gunfighter's mind as to how this contest might turn out – and if he had doubts, then that gave Jed a sliver of hope.

Faces had appeared at windows and doorways all along the main street of Paradise. The good folks of the town were being treated to a spectacle they had never seen before and would likely never see again, so most of those faces displayed expressions of awe and excitement. This was an occasion they were going to make the most of.

Jed had become inexplicably calm from the second Ryker had first opened his mouth, and if he was about to die at that man's hand, then neither his body nor his mind was aware of it. For him it felt like his whole life had been building up to this one moment in time, and he was soon to discover whether that moment would bring him life or death.

Brad Ryker's eyelid fluttered wildly again, and a bead of sweat ran down his forehead and along the length of his nose to make the long trip to the dusty street at the gunman's feet. Jed just wished he would hurry up and

154

make his play – the hot sun was beating down mercilessly on the back of his unprotected neck, and the front of his shirt was wet through from sweat.

All of a sudden Jed saw Ryker's gun hand sweep upwards in a graceful motion. It was fast, and it was controlled, but Jed's hand had found the butt of his Navy Colt just as quick as Ryker's found the butt of his six-gun, and both men had their weapons clear of their holsters in unison, Jed thumbing back the hammer on his a split second ahead of Ryker, and the resultant boom created when the hammer crashed back down rattling the windows of the stores either side of the street.

Brad Ryker got a shot off, too. But not before Jed's bullet had struck him just below the ribcage, causing him to miss his aim and send a load of lead over Jed's right shoulder. Not hesitating for a second, Jed brought the hammer back on his Colt for a second time, and taking better aim this time, made certain he would be the one walking away by punching a hole clean through Ryker's forehead.

Brad Ryker immediately dropped his pistol and took two shuffling steps forwards. He hadn't been in this position before: it was always him holding the smoking gun and the other fellow struggling to maintain his footing. With a sickening gurgle from deep within his chest he brought up a sudden rush of blood that gushed from his mouth and coloured his shiny black boots a deep shade of crimson.

Jed lowered his Colt and became nothing more than a bystander as he watched the man who had tried to take his life stagger several feet towards him and then collapse in spectacular fashion a few yards away. Brad Ryker the feared gunfighter had fought his last battle.

CHAPTER SIXTEEN

Knocking gently on the door of the room at the Silver Dollar Saloon, Jed waited patiently for its occupant to cross the floor and open up to him. 'Hello, Laney,' he said, when the startled beauty peeped nervously through the crack at him. 'I've come to see how you are.'

The door swung wide open and she stood there looking at him as if she were seeing a ghost.

'Aren't you going to invite me in?'

'I thought you had left for Wyoming,' she said totally befuddled.

'I was about to, but I heard what Brad Ryker did to you, so decided to hang around long enough to make sure he never touches you again.'

Her eyes widened at the revelation. 'You haven't gone and challenged him, have you?'

He nodded.

'Jed, he'll kill you. Please don't do this on my account. I'm not worth dying for.'

Reaching out his hand he placed his palm very

gently against her bruised face. 'I happen to think you are.' He smiled at her then. 'Ryker's dead, Laney. He wasn't quite as fast on the draw as he thought he was. At least, he wasn't quite as fast as me.'

She struggled to take it in. 'You drew on him? Is that the commotion I heard down in the street half an hour ago?'

He nodded again.

'Oh, Jed, you are foolish. If he had killed you I would never have forgiven myself.'

He allowed a small grin to part his lips. 'That's a fine thank-you, I must say.'

Not waiting for an invitation Laney Landers slid her arms around him and snuggled in close, and despite his fear of suffering a repeat of the fiasco with Belinda, Jed Grayson had no desire to try and stop her.

'I wish you weren't leaving for Wyoming,' she said, a sudden sob slipping unexpectedly from her.

'I wish I could take you to Wyoming with me,' he admitted.

Pulling away she looked up at him. 'Then why don't you?'

'What. . . ?'

'Why don't you take me to Wyoming with you?'

'Because you won't want to live on a ranch.'

Placing her hands on her curvy hips she stared at him in disbelief for a moment. 'Jed Grayson, when did I ever tell you I didn't want to live on a ranch?'

'You've never lived on a ranch in your life. You're a town gal.'

'I'll have you know I was raised on a ranch, and if Ma

and Pa hadn't died when I was only fourteen I'd be there still. My aunt sold it out from underneath me and ran off with all the money. That's how I ended up singing and dancing to try and make ends meet.'

'So you have no objection to living on a ranch, then?'

'None whatsoever.'

Jed's mind raced. He could play this safe and walk away from this woman and not run the risk of getting his heart broken again, or he could roll the dice and give a relationship with her a whirl. The thing was, he got a strong feeling that if he chose the former he was going to end up with a broken heart anyway.

'Laney Landers,' he said, deciding to throw caution to the wind, 'will you marry me?'

She smiled at him despite it hurting her battered face. 'Of course I will, Jed Grayson.'

He kissed her then, and for the first time in many years he willingly gave his heart away.

Jed hung around in Paradise until Laney had healed well enough so they could get married. The wedding and reception was put on for them by none other than Thomas Thornton himself. Although Rebecca was stung by the suddenness of it all, she took it like the true lady that she was, and wished the newly married couple a long and happy marriage. Jed had his suspicions it wouldn't be long before she would be getting married herself. Jack Wilson had confessed to him that he had held a torch for the young woman for quite some time, but had never had the opportunity to be alone with her – but the way the two had danced and laughed together at the wedding reception he could see that the Thorntons' foreman had finally managed to make rather an impression on her.

Thomas Thornton provided Jed with a buckboard and ample provisions to get himself and his new bride to Wyoming, saying it was the least he could do for the man who had saved his ranch for him. He then elicited a promise from the young couple that they would come back for a visit before too long, and as the pair were about to pull out of the Thornton's barnyard to begin their journey, he slipped Jed an envelope containing two thousand dollars in cash.

Waving over their shoulders, Mr and Mrs Grayson guided the buckboard up the slope to the road, travelling back to the spot from which Jed had looked down on the town on that fateful day of his arrival. He then pulled up the two horses and smiled at his new wife.

'What. . . ?' she asked, curious as to why he had stopped and was looking at her in the way he was.

He smiled lovingly at her. 'This marriage is bound to be a success because I met my sweetheart in Paradise, and isn't Paradise where everything's perfect?' Then with a flick of the reins and a 'hey-up' to the team, he headed for Wyoming, eager to show off his beautiful new bride to his uncle.